<u>Praise for the award-w</u>
<u>mystery ......</u>

"Joe Cosentino has a unique and fabulous gift. His writing is flawless, and his use of farce, along with his convoluted plot-lines, will have you guessing until the very last page, which makes his books a joy to read. His books are worth their weight in gold, and if you haven't discovered them yet you are in for a rare treat." — *Divine Magazine*

"a combination of Laurel and Hardy mixed with Hitchcock and *Murder She Wrote*...Loaded with puns and one-liners...Right to the end, you are kept guessing, and the conclusion still has a surprise in store for you." — *Optimumm Book Reviews*

"adventure, mystery, and romance with every page....Funny, clever, and sweet....I can't find anything not to love about this series....This read had me laughing and falling in love....Nicky and Noah are my favorite gay couple." — *Urban Book Reviews*

"For fans of Joe Cosentino's hilarious mysteries, this is another vintage story with more cheeky asides and sub plots right left and centre....The story is fast paced, funny and sassy. The writing is very witty with lots of tongue-in-cheek humour....Highly recommended." — *Boy Meets Boy Reviews*

"This delightfully sudsy, colorful cast of characters would rival that of any daytime soap opera, and the character exchanges are rife with sass, wit and cagey sarcasm....As the pages turn quickly, the author keeps us hanging until the startling end." — *Edge Media Network*

Books by Joe Cosentino

Drama

Queen

A Nicky and Noah Mystery

Joe Cosentino

Cover art by Jesús Da Silva
Nicky & Noah Logo by Holly McCabe
Cover and interior design by Fred Wolinsky

To Fred for everything,
and to everyone who inhabits
the world of academia.

CAST OF CHARACTERS

The Theatre Professors at Treemeadow College:
Nicky Abbondanza: Professor of Play Directing
Noah Oliver: Professor of Acting
Martin Anderson: Professor of Theatre Management/Theatre Department Head
Jackson Grier: Professor of Stage Movement
Ariella Samson: Professor of Costuming
David Samson: Professor of Technical Theatre
Loptu Lee: Professor of Playwriting
Millie Rodriguez: Professor of Voice and Diction
Wally Wanker: Emeritus Professor of Voice and Diction

Theatre Graduate Assistants:
Scotty Bruno: Nicky's graduate assistant
Tyler Thompson: David's graduate assistant

Theatre Office Assistant:
Shayla Johnson

Theatre Students/Leads of Nicky's Play:
David Amour
Jan Annondale
Kayla Calloway
Ricky Gonzalez

Film Students:
Kyle Samson
P.J. Myers

Film Professor:
Faith O'Riley

Human Resource:
Mickey Minor

Detectives:
Jose Manuello: Senior Detective
John Dickerson: Junior Detective

We'll Never Tell:
Butch Whopper
Reg McCallister

CHAPTER ONE

Surrounded by darkness, I sat tensely watching as a young, beautiful man lay on the floor with blood dripping off his six-pack abs. I held my breath. Another muscular young man stood over the first and looked down with a vengeful gaze and devious smirk. My heart pounded as he strutted through the quiet street in his long flowing cape, weaving from corpse to corpse. His knife, erect, poised. "The Lord is vengeful and strong in wrath. And revenge is oh so sweet," he said.

"Blackout then lights up!"

Tyler, the technical theatre graduate assistant running the lighting board, hit a button, and our Treemeadow College theatre once again sported its Victorian proscenium, cream-colored walls, maple wood wainscoting, bronze wall sconces, and ruby red stage curtain.

Sitting behind the director's desk (actually a wooden plank temporarily set up in the center of the audience seating area) I scribbled a last note before shouting, "Good work, everyone! Please get out of costume and make-up as quickly as possible and join me in the first two rows of the house for notes."

Students scurried about: the actors off the stage; the technicians behind the set securing lighting and prop pieces.

Since it is tech week for my show, I have been working in our Edwardian style theatre every evening alongside our workaholic technical director. Tyler Thompson is our technical theatre professor's graduate assistant, who like all good technical directors, eats, sleeps, breathes, and basically lives in our Scene Shop behind the stage. Standing at five feet tall with mountainous shoulders, a broad back, powerful arms, thick hands, and stick legs, Tyler rules over all things sound, lights, projections, set pieces, and props at Treemeadow College. When he leaves, we will be at a total loss to find or do anything technical in our theatre.

Sets for plays used to consist of wooden flats screwed together to create the walls of a room or a slide projection of a building. Nowadays no set is worth its weight in a Tony Award if it doesn't include moving film projections of farmland, urban settings, fireworks, or whatever exterior is called for in a given scene.

"I'll fix the video of the street scene for tomorrow night, Nicky." Tyler slumped in a chair next to me as the familiar smell of pepperoni, his staple food, and sawdust stung my nose. He wore his usual techie attire: a soiled white T-shirt under frayed overalls above worn workboats. This *look* was accented by a gold cross around his neck, tattoos on his arms (like an illustrated book with words, numbers, and pictures), and long, stringy, unwashed hair. Tyler scratched at his beard, a result of him not having shaved (or washed) since we started tech. "I also want to fix the sound cue for the siren, and change a few gels for the red wash across the stage during the murders."

Before I could thank Tyler, David Samson, Professor of Technical Theatre and our show's Scenic Designer, barreled down the theatre aisle like a bull in a field of tomatoes, shouting, "Tyler!" David is an imposing six feet two inches tall, weighing about a hundred and eighty pounds with a shaved head.

Tyler froze, and replied like a convicted chemical dumper facing an environmental lynch mob. "Yes, David?"

"You didn't add in the new light cue I gave you for the top of Act II."

"I'll have it for tomorrow night," Tyler said.

David's strong features hardened. "Your procrastination and laziness are not acceptable." He scowled. "Do it *now*."

"Sure, David," Tyler responded as he leapt off the theatre seat and hurried into the Lighting booth at the back of the theatre.

I came to Tyler's defense. "David, Tyler has done an amazing job—"

"Nicky, the pacing of the show is too slow. The blocking isn't balanced. The actors aren't committing fully to their roles and to listening to one another. This comes as no surprise to me since our Acting professor is as incompetent as *you* are, Nicky, as our Directing professor. Unfortunately, it seems you'd rather flirt with one another than get to work! This is a disgrace to our department!" David raised his arms in the air like a preacher facing an unrepentant congregation. "*You're* the director, Nicky. And I use that term lightly. Your other shows have been insulting to the intelligence of the audience, but *this* one has reached the pinnacle of being even *worse*! Will even *you* let an audience see this repugnant *crap*?"

"David, this is not the time or place to have this discussion."

With the student actors and technicians sitting in the front of the theatre (obliviously texting on their phones), my student stage manager, SuCho, screamed for everyone's attention, and for me to come to the front of the theatre house to give them my notes. This thankfully sent David off to his office in a huff.

After I had given my first few notes, I noticed Noah Oliver standing in the back of the theatre. Noah is tall and lean with curly blond hair, blue eyes, and the sweetest smile I have ever wanted to kiss in an Assistant Professor. While I teach Theatre History and Play Directing, Noah is our department's specialist in Acting, and for good reason. Noah is a terrific actor, a creative and passionate teacher, and a wonderful colleague. More importantly, I have had a crush on him since the moment he made his entrance into our humble campus three years ago. Noah is single, gay, and seems to really like me. Why don't I ask him out? Noah is twenty-eight years young. As a junior professor in my department in need of my vote for tenure this year, if I make a pass at him it could be considered attempted coercion on my part.

It was difficult for me to concentrate on giving my notes to the students since Scotty Bruno, my graduate assistant and Assistant Director of the play, was talking, laughing, and obviously flirting with Noah in the rear of the theatre. I had reason to be concerned. Scotty has bleached blond hair, contact lens turquoise eyes, ultra-white bonded teeth, and muscles as if sculpted by Michelangelo, housed in multi-colored, stuffed shorts and tank top (in winter) that were not unnoticed by Noah. Unless I was becoming nearsighted, I could have sworn that Scotty whispered something into Noah's ear then handed Noah a box. *What the heck is in it? Love letters? Condoms? My heart on a silver platter?*

"Any notes for me, Professor?" Paul Amour, my leading man, sat front row center and winked at me. Identifying as bisexual, Paul uses his *charms* with men and women alike to get their attention. Tall with shiny, wavy black hair climbing down his neck, chiseled features, and a body like a Greek god, getting attention wasn't too difficult for Paul.

"You were like terrific tonight, Paul. I really believed you were like the murderer!" Ricky Gonzalez, Paul's co-star and last onstage murder victim, sat next to Paul like an art dealer admiring the Mona Lisa. Ricky is shorter and darker than Paul with a smaller but equally cut physique. After he graduates from college and gets over his crush on Paul, Ricky will no doubt make some guy a wonderful husband.

"Thanks, Ricky." Paul squeezed one of Ricky's abdominal muscles.

Ricky beamed like a floodlight.

Kayla Calloway and Jan Annondale, who play murder victims one and two in the play, sat on the other side of Paul to reward their peripheral visions. Zaftig, giggly, and insecure, they hung on Paul's every word, wishing they could hang on Paul.

"Your fight scenes were totally awesome tonight, Paul," said Kayla.

Jan added, "And you really like aced your cool monologue at the end of the play."

Before Paul could sign autographs, I said, "I have five more pages of notes tonight, people. Can I have everyone's attention?"

As the cast members groaned I noticed that Noah and Scotty had left the theatre (to have a quickie in the lobby?). The students listened while I gave notes for improvement on their diction, movements, timing, reacting on stage (or lack thereof), character development, and emotional levels. After my last note, the students presented me with a blueberry cheesecake (thanks to the organic dairy farm bordering the college), singing "Happy Birthday" in four-part harmony (the lesbians at the lower notes and the gay men hitting the high notes). I was filled with gratitude until I noticed the thirty-five candles on top of the cake (obviously leaked to my students by Eve Harrington, my graduate assistant Scotty Bruno).

Allow me to break the fourth wall a moment—

This is the twentieth play that I have directed. Half of them were prior to my becoming a college professor, meaning when I had a low salary, no benefits, and no job security. Thankfully the fates led me to nabbing the coveted brass ring: a tenure track Assistant Professor position in the Theatre Department at a small, private New England college. This ultimately led to tenure and Associate Professor status with all the benefits it entails (salary, house, medical insurance, pension) and a hopeful promotion to full Professor next year.

My name is Nicky Abbondanza, PHD. The PHD (as an ex-boyfriend used to say before he left me for his life coach) stands for perky, hot, and adorable. He wasn't much of a speller. My parents told me that my brother got the looks and I got the brains. Since my brother looks like Margaret Thatcher, I wasn't too hopeful about my academic future.

Thankfully I was a straight B+ student and enjoyed writing academic papers such as "The All Male Acting Ensemble of the Elizabethan Theatre," "Shakespeare's Sonnets to His Mystery Male Lover," and "Christopher Marlowe's Secret

Husband."

Because you, gentle reader, are always curious what your leads look like...well, I am over six-feet tall with straight black hair, green eyes, Roman nose, and an average to muscular build; meaning I go to the gym when I'm between boyfriends. I go to the gym a lot. And I'll come right out and say that I have a huge penis. You might think this an idle boast — doesn't everyone claim to be well-endowed these days, as if rulers aren't standard measurements. The truth is my flaccid penis is nine and a quarter inches long and two inches wide. This is according to an ex-boyfriend who measured it while I was writing my dissertation. This blessing, or curse, back in high school caused teasing in the locker room: "Hey, it's the original foot-long wiener!" At least they didn't tease me for being gay. It has also solicited numerous more recent calls for "a viewing" at the gym. Finally, it has led to either great joy or incredible horror for anyone who dates me. I know what you are thinking. I should become a porn star. No thanks. I'll keep my day (and night) job at the college. I don't even watch porn, except in the evenings when I'm not working, during the day if I'm sick or depressed, on weekends, and during holidays.

Coming from Kansas, I truly am a friend of Dorothy's who has settled down in Treemeadow, a little college town in Vermont, surrounded by snowcapped mountain landscapes dotted with white church steeples, quaint covered bridges over babbling brooks, and a warm and cozy fireplace burning next to a rainbow flag seen through the window of the LGBT bookstore.

Now, back to my story —

"Thirty-five! Professor, you are well preserved for someone so old."

"I hope I'm still working at thirty-five."

To Paul and Ricky, and to all of my students, thirty-five is older than Methuselah.

"The first one back with a piece can feed *me*," said Paul

with a bad boy grin.

"No food in the theatre." After laying down the law, SuCho yanked open the theatre doors and the students filed out into the lobby.

Ariella, our Professor of Costuming and the costume designer for the play (with costumes hanging over both arms) carefully made her way off the stage and gave me a kiss on the cheek.

"Happy birthday, Nicky."

"So you've heard I'm ancient...and incompetent."

Flicking back her long, black hair, Ariella said in her usual monotone, "Don't let the kids get to you, Nicky. And don't let David get to you either. The show is terrific."

I unleashed a half smile. "Tell David that."

"I already did. Right after his tirade about the 'pedestrian and mundane' costumes. Nicky, David doesn't like anything, except David." *Are there tears brimming in her dark eyes?* "Nobody knows that better than me."

"Ariella, I hope this isn't too personal, but with all of your complaints about David, why do you stay married to him?"

She offered a bitter smile. "That my friend is a very good question."

Ariella went to the Costume Shop adjacent to the stage. I joined the students who were scattered throughout the theatre lobby licking their plastic forks clean of cheesecake while texting each other in dismay over the rising tuition at the college.

Paul, Ricky, Kayla, and Jan sat on the flared stairway leading to the balcony. Kayla, a beautiful dark-skinned African American, and Jan, a gorgeous pale-skinned Albino, were on either side of olive-skinned Ricky as if forming a three-layer cake. Paul faced them and appeared to be presenting some type of proposal. Since they are the officers of the Theatre Club on campus, I assumed they were discussing club business. As I am the club's faculty advisor I walked over, leaned on a gold marble column, and overheard their conversation.

Jan whispered, "I don't know if I can um go through with this, guys."

Paul arched his massive back and slipped his muscular arm around her quivering shoulder, "Sure you can, Jan. Trust me. I'll take care of everything."

As Jan melted, Kayla combed her hair and giggled. "It could be like fun."

With eyes only for Paul, Ricky said, "If you um want me to do it, Paul, I'm in."

I made my way to the gold staircase railing and asked if they needed my help.

"No thanks, Professor, we're cool," said Paul with a contraction and release of his pectoral muscles to the delight of his cohorts.

"Cool cake, professor." Kayla and Jan giggled as they each fed a piece to Paul.

Ricky added with a smirk, "Paul and I can like drive you home if you are too old to drive, Professor."

I grimaced. "Very funny."

I left my students to their private discussion and joined my young graduate assistant seated on a red velvet bench in a turreted area of the lobby. As I dug into my sizable piece of cake, Scotty leaned into me like a cat facing a sardine, "Since it looks like the tech rehearsal will run late, I can teach your morning Theatre History class tomorrow."

"That won't be necessary, Scotty." *Just stick your finger down your throat then head to the gym as usual.*

"With teaching your classes, assessing and updating curriculum, going to faculty meetings, advising students, writing your articles, advising the theatre club, and directing plays, I worry that you may get sick."

You'd unleash the bubonic plague if it meant getting my job. I patted his shaved and oiled knee, and said a la Margo Channing, "I'm fine, Scotty. Just leave your notes on tonight's performance in my office box tomorrow."

"Am I too late for the party?" My knees dipped as Noah Oliver took off his coat and scarf and stood next to me.

"Happy birthday, Nicky!" He winked at me.

Maybe we can adopt seven children, run away to the hills, and start a family singing act.

Scotty leapt from his seat like it was a pogo stick. "Have a piece of cake, Noah. No nuts!"

I beg your pardon?

"Thanks for remembering, Scotty." Noah sat between Scotty and me and dug into the creamy wonder. *Was that a familiar smile between Scotty and Noah?!*

Scotty explained as if he was Noah's husband, "Noah is allergic to nuts, Nicky."

Hopefully not to mine.

Noah took me in with his baby blue eyes. *Did I notice a look of lust in them?* "How's the show going?"

What show? Oh! "We're all exhausted, frazzled, panicked, and certain of a great opening night."

Noah squeezed my hand. "You're an amazing director. The creative way you move your characters around the stage, how the elements of design compliment the story, and your unique vision is thrilling to watch. I expect nothing short of brilliance in this production." Noah beamed with pride. "*And* you have some powerful student actors in the show."

Scotty collected our empty plates. "Noah is a terrific acting teacher." He gazed at Noah with pure adoration. "The students are lucky to have you."

Since theatre is a collaborative art, I said, "Tyler's execution of David's scenic design is amazing, and as usual Tyler has been a total work horse. Ariella's costumes have an incredible gothic look, but they're light enough for the students to move around in them."

Noah whispered in my ear, and I restrained myself from throwing myself on top of him. "Can I speak to you about something...personal?"

"Sure." *How about a June wedding?*

While Scotty stared at us with an inquisitive look on his face, Noah led me to a window seat in a corner of the theatre lobby. White snow fell softly outside the window behind us like cotton bits in a glass ball. I could tell something was bothering Noah, and it hurt me that he was hurting.

"I don't want to take advantage of our friendship."

Take advantage! "What's wrong?"

"It's about my tenure application."

I thought back to the neurosis, prayers, nightmares, and sheer terror before my tenure decision. "Noah, anybody lucky enough to get a tenure track position nowadays goes through the jitters stage. It's not fun, but it's part of the game. I read your application. It's very strong. All the students and all the faculty in the department like you."

His head dropped to his chest. "Not everybody."

David, the self-prescribed technical theatre god, strikes again.

"I went to David's office while you were giving notes."

Tongue firmly in cheek, I said, "And the two of you had a cozy little chat about your promising future at Treemeadow College?"

Noah let out an *I Love Lucy,* "Hah!" then continued. "After complimenting David on the set design for the show, I mentioned my positive student surveys, and my supportive evaluations from Martin as department head."

"And when you asked if he will support your tenure, David said he'd have to think about it." I sneered. "That's what David said to me when I applied for tenure." I felt my jaw, hands, and knees clench in unison. "His was my only no vote, which I will *never* forget."

"I fared worse than you. David came right out and told me I am too easy on my students, and that like most gay men I am too *weak* to be a dynamic lecturer."

"That's a lie. And against the *law* in this state."

Noah's magnificent lips pouted. "David told me that he wouldn't support my tenure if I gave him a thousand dollars."

"He's never supported *anyone* for tenure. He has voted against every new course and program modification proposal in the department. He even voted against having a department holiday party. But David's is only *one* vote."

Resting his warm hand on my grateful shoulder, Noah said, "Nicky, David is running for department head."

"He won't win against Martin."

Slumping back against the window seat, Noah said, "There are only seven tenured faculty members in our department. David can be very persuasive."

"Ariella may be David's wife but she's her own person, and she likes you a great deal. And I doubt Jackson Grier would support David since David voted against Jackson's tenure too."

"I heard Jackson and David arguing in David's office tonight before I went in to talk to David about my tenure. Jackson slammed the door and left in a huff."

"What were David and Jackson arguing about?"

Noah shrugged. "I heard David criticizing Jackson's movement and stage combat choreography for the show. Then all I could get were the words, 'fresh start.'" Soft lines surfaced on Noah's handsome face. "David could be making deals, offering his support to faculty if he becomes department head *and* if they vote against my tenure."

I stood and lifted Noah to his feet. "Come on, young man."

He looked like a school boy at a fire drill. "Where are we going?"

"Where everyone in our department brings all of our problems."

A delicious line formed between Noah's eyes. "Is Martin here at this hour?"

"My bet is *yes*."

I pushed Noah in front of me, and said grandly, "To the Wizard of Theatre Arts."

A few minutes later we were in the white stone building next door, which houses our faculty offices, lab theatre, rehearsal hall, and classrooms. Martin was just about to leave his office when Noah and I arrived like the Scarecrow and the Tin Man asking for our special wish.

Our department head is a short, thin, balding man who looks like Pinocchio, if Pinocchio was in his sixties. Besides being a terrific Theatre Management professor, Martin is honest, kind, incredibly competent, and a tireless advocate for everyone and everything in our department. When I grow up, I want to be Martin Anderson.

"Nicky! Noah! Come in. Have a seat." Pretending he hadn't been on his way home, Martin surreptitiously slipped off his hat and coat then settled us all on tall, leather wingback chairs around his cherry wood mantel fireplace with china cups filled with hot cocoa in our hands and monogrammed cranberry cloth napkins on our knees. Martin wore his usual wardrobe of a white button-down shirt, black pants, and matching sweater vest and bowtie (cranberry today).

I said, "Working on next term's budget?"

Martin smiled revealing jagged teeth from biting on too many number two pencils. "The budget, course schedule, and curriculum reports for next term are finished. I was going over student grade appeals."

Noah's jaw dropped. "It's only February. Grade appeals so soon?"

I patted Noah on the head, and said a la W.C. Fields, "The way our students are coddled at home and in high school, there are always grade appeals, my boy." I took a sip of my sweet cocoa, and asked Martin, "Doesn't Ruben ever complain about the hours you keep at the college?"

Martin smiled at the picture of him and his husband on his large cherry wood desk. "After over forty years together, we understand each other's passions...for one another *and* for our work."

Ruben is the C.E.O. of a gay rights organization, a devoted husband to Martin, and a loving father to their two adopted children, now grown women with families of their own.

"But enough about me. How's the show coming?"

"I'll let you know after opening night...and after I sleep about twenty-four hours."

"You do terrific work...both of you."

"Thanks."

Martin looked like a termite in a wood shed. "Now tell me

everything that is going on at rehearsals. Any love affairs among the students? Arguments between the staff? Artistic tempers flaring?"

Besides being an amazing department head, Martin is also an amazing gossip. Though he will keep any secret asked of him in confidence, everything else is fair game for a major Martin chin wag.

I filled Martin in on the latest antics of my cast and crew, including Ricky, Kayla, and Jan's infatuation with my play's leading man.

After I ran out of gossip, Noah said tensely, "Martin, we came to see you about David Samson." Noah rested a shaky elbow on the arm of his chair. "Besides Ariella, who in our department might be swayed by him?"

Martin's eyes twinkled like the Big Dipper. "I doubt Loptu would be...*any longer.*"

That peaked my interest. "What does Loptu have against David?"

Martin salivated over each word. "Well, they were once...*an item.*"

I couldn't believe our split personality Playwriting professor was once David's mistress. "How do you know?"

"Loptu was in here weeping and wailing when David dumped her last week. I held her hand and let her cry on my shoulder..." he grinned, "...while I got the whole story out of her."

Unleashing his warm heart, Noah asked, "How is Loptu now?"

"Fine, thanks to a steady supply of little red, blue, and green psychotropic wonders from her psychiatrist."

"Does Ariella know about David and Loptu?" I asked.

Martin giggled merrily. "How could Ariella *not* know? We are a very small community here at Treemeadow." Back to Noah's question, Martin said, "However, Millie will probably do *anything* David asks."

My jaw dropped to the cocoa stain on the carpet. "Millie and David are *together*?"

Martin was nearly orgasmic. "They are *glued* together like a televangelist and his wig."

Noticing the look of fear on Noah's face, I said, "As our Voice and Diction professor, Millie is Noah's closest colleague. Regardless of her affair with David, she would *never* do anything to hurt Noah."

"What's this about?" asked Martin at the edge of his seat.

I stood by my man, or rather by the man I wished was my man. "Tonight David told Noah that he isn't supporting Noah's tenure application."

Martin laughed. "Big news. David has never supported anyone or anything."

I nodded. "But David said some untrue and probably illegal things to Noah."

Martin's curiosity was peeked, a relatively easy task. I filled Martin in on the latest *words of wisdom* from David to Noah.

When I was finished, Noah's leg shook nervously, as he said, "My concern is that David might try to poison others in the department against me, and use his running for department head as leverage."

Martin seemed to grow a foot in stature. "David's a bully. And the only way to deal with a bully is to stand up to him." Looking like a mother bear facing a hunter, Martin added, "David tells me that everything I do is wrong. Well, now I will do something that is right." He put his hand on Noah's shoulder. "And I promise we won't lose you, Noah." Martin put his arms around us and walked us to the door. "The people in this department mean more to me than you know. I won't stand idly by when a fox gets into my hen house." We stopped at the door. Martin looked at us like a father sending his children off to bed. "Go home. Get some rest. And let *me* take care of David."

After thanking Martin, Noah and I did exactly that. Unfortunately, each in our own beds.

* * *

I woke the next morning to the local news blaring from the radio alarm on my night table. Before I could hit the snooze button, I heard the news announcer's top story. "Early this morning David Samson, Professor of Technical Theatre, was found dead in his office at Treemeadow College with a knife lodged in his back."

Chapter Two

"David Samson is dead at fifty-one years old."

As Detective Manuello announced this, I couldn't help thinking, *It's not only the good who die young.* Having showered, eaten breakfast, taken my vitamins, and driven to the college in thirty minutes flat, I was in my maple wood paneled office between my classes. Our graduate assistants, Tyler and Scotty, were teaching David's classes for the day as well as giving David's students the news.

I sat behind my oak desk looking over the tops of play scripts and class rosters at Detective Manuello sitting to my left and Detective Dickerson sitting to my right. Playing the role of bad cop, Detective Manuello had a permanent scowl on his probably once handsome face as he ran his chubby fingers through his graying hair. The unwavering smile on Detective Dickerson's still unlined face, not to mention his ginger hair, freckles, and swimmer's build, cast him in the role of good cop. As a seasoned theatre director, I wasn't totally buying either performance.

Bursting out of the middle of his dark suit, Detective Manuello scratched at the massive stomach hanging over his belt, and asked, "Professor Abbondanza, were you and Professor Samson close?"

Not if I could help it. "David designed the set for my current play, detective."

Filling his dark suit nicely, Detective Dickerson smiled and nodded like Howdy Doody. "You guys put on great plays here at the college. I've seen *all* of them."

I could never hear enough praise from a fan. "Thank you,

detective. I'll make sure you get two complimentary tickets for opening night."

"Terrific. Thank you!" Dickerson looked about ready to ask for my autograph.

Manuello looked at Dickerson like John Wilkes Booth facing Lincoln in his box seat then said, "Professor Abbondanza, we spoke to Professor Samson's graduate assistant..." He looked at his notes. "...Tyler Thompson, who confirmed that the knife used at the end of your play was the same knife the cleaning woman found early this morning in Professor Samson's back. How did the knife get into Professor Samson's office?"

My pulse quickened. "How should *I* know? *I* didn't put it there." *Could I possibly sound guiltier?*

It seemed like Detective Manuello wanted to put a knife in *my* back. "Don't you usually use a *fake* knife in your stage productions?"

Detective Dickerson sighed. "I remember that great death scene in your production of *Macbeth*!"

I opened my desk drawer, popped a fist full of vitamins into my mouth, and took a swig of water from a bottle buried under a stack of class reading lists on my desk. Since I frequently didn't have the time to eat right, and I occasionally had a streak of hypochondria (like needing to review my will each time I get a cold), I swallow lots of vitamins.

"We use a fake knife for the fight scenes and stabbing scenes. Since the knife is in motion, it not only provides safety for the actors, but it's also harder for the audience to see that it's a fake. When the murderer stands still holding the knife, as in the closing scene in this production, we use a real knife, so it glimmers realistically under the stage lights."

"I can't wait to experience it," said Dickerson.

From the hungry look on Dickerson's face, it appeared that he wanted to experience *me.*

Manuello shot dagger eyes at Dickerson, and asked, "And whose idea was it to use a real knife?"

"I believe it was our movement director's idea."

Manuello readied his pencil onto his pad. "And your movement director's name, Professor?"

"Jackson. Professor of Movement and Stage Combat Jackson Grier." *Why do I feel like a stool pigeon in a 1940's detective movie?*

Dickerson piped up again. "I really enjoyed Professor Grier's all-movement production of *The Frogs* at the college last year. Grier has a real flare for creating interesting human pictures on stage."

Manuello cleared his throat and again readied his pencil. "Professor, what happened to the *real* knife after your technical rehearsal last night?"

I thought back. "I assume it was put back on the prop table backstage."

"By whom?"

"By the student in charge of props."

Manuello wrote on his pad. "Was anyone else near the prop table during that time?"

"Sure. Lots of people," I said.

Again Dickerson interjected. "With productions as technically complicated as yours, Professor, I'll bet you have lots of people on your technical staff."

If the knife had been in my office at that moment, I think Manuello would have used it on his partner. Instead Manuello turned his glare toward me, and asked, "Can you be more specific?"

I had lost track of our conversation. "About...?"

Manuello looked like he wanted to commit double murder. "Who had access to the knife, the *real* knife, *after* your rehearsal last night?"

I leaned forward as if giving a class lecture. "Our student stage manager, all the students in the cast and crew, our technical director—that is David's graduate assistant Tyler Thompson who you mentioned earlier, *my* graduate assistant Scotty Bruno, our costume designer professor Ariella Samson—"

Trying to wrap up the interview before his partner asked

if he could audition for my next production, Manuello asked, "Professor, who else was in the theatre building, and in your department's adjoining building, last night?"

I thought back again. "Let's see, our department head, Martin Anderson, was in his office."

"How do you know that?"

"Noah and I...Assistant Professor of Acting Noah Oliver and I went to see Professor Anderson after the rehearsal."

"About what?"

"To discuss Noah's tenure application."

Dickerson nearly leapt off his seat. "Oliver is a terrific acting teacher."

Manuello could no longer contain himself. "And just how would *you* know that, Dickerson?"

Undaunted, Detective Dickerson answered, "My wife took an evening acting class with Professor Oliver and she *really* enjoyed it."

Since Dickerson was staring at my crotch like a teenager facing a fake ID, I surmised what *he* was doing while his wife took evening classes at the college.

Manuello's sour face turned toward me again. "Does everyone in your department support Professor Oliver's tenure?"

I spoke without thinking: "I believe everyone does, except for the murder victim." *We'll get married before Noah goes to prison. I'll hide a nail file in my socks during a conjugal visit.*

Manuello made a note. "Was anyone else still here last night?"

I thought hard, grasping at every straw in the box called my head. "Noah said that Jackson...Professor Grier had visited David in David's office."

"I'll bet Grier's fight scenes are amazingly realistic in this show!" Dickerson said like a paid-off critic.

Manuello asked Dickerson to wait outside in the car for him. Like a puppy caught making a mess on the rug, Dickerson retrieved his trench coat from my office coat rack and left the room.

"Professor Abbondanza, do you mind if I take your fingerprints? I am asking everyone in your department."

"Sure, I don't want to be the only one not invited to the party."

Detective Manuello didn't share my sense of humor. As he smudged my fingers into his ink pad and pressed them onto a card with my name written on it, he asked, "Did you like Professor Samson?"

I tried diplomacy. "I felt the same way about David Samson as everyone else did in my department."

"Which is?"

"He was a gifted technical designer," I answered truthfully.

"And as a *person*?"

I stared at the brick fireplace across from my desk, trying to decide if I should throw myself into it.

"Be honest. Whatever you don't tell me I can find out elsewhere."

Wiping the ink off my hands with a paper towel, I decided to come clean. "All right, detective. The truth is David Samson was a bully, a sadist, and a tyrant. I despised the ground he walked on, and he didn't care much for me either. He had a knack for finding everyone's weak spot then going for the jugular."

Manuello thanked me for my candor, and for my fingerprints. After he put his trench coat over his arm and left my office, I sat staring at the PHD plaque on my office wall, wondering why I didn't become a plumber.

After lecturing to my Directing I class about the importance of character analysis in a play, I divided the students into groups of four with the instructions to analyze the leading characters in their group's assigned play then report their findings to the rest of the class. The students usually begin group work by texting and complaining about the assignment, and about the high cost of tuition. I wasn't surprised when they instead began talking about the murder on campus. Thankfully, as I walked from group to group, they settled down to interesting discussions about the backgrounds, desires, fears, and psyches of the characters in their plays.

When I came to Paul Amour's group, composed of the leading actors from my play, I overheard their conversation.

Jan stood in the center of the group, and whispered, "I can't believe we like actually did it."

"I don't have any um guilt about it," said Kayla with an upraised chin.

Paul stretched his muscular arms, and said, "Given the situation, it was something we *had* to do."

Gazing at Paul, Ricky said, "I'm glad we like did it."

Are they talking about the assignment, or about something else? Since their assigned play turned out to be about two serial killers falling in love with two prostitutes, I gave them the benefit of the doubt.

Disturbing the class by coming in late, as usual, P.J. Myers pulled at one of his pierced eyebrows, apologized for being late then joined a group. At the end of class I noticed P.J. giving something to Jan and Jan thanking him before hurrying off with Paul, Ricky, and Kayla. Watching P.J.'s crestfallen face after Jan left, I came to the conclusion that there was a dramatic plotline happening in this class separate from my improvisation assignment.

Walking back to my office after class, I overheard giggling coming from Noah's office next door. My legs and ears took on a life of their own as I found myself in front of Noah's door with my ear pressed against it. I figured out quickly that the two voices belonged to Noah and my graduate assistant, Scotty.

"Now that I'm a faculty member, you and I can hang out more often, Noah," said my graduate assistant coyly.

Noah responded, "You and Tyler are teaching David's classes on a *temporary* basis, Scotty."

After another giggle. "I might be able to make it *permanent.*"

Over my dead body. Wait a minute!

"Don't worry," Scotty continued seductively, "I won't tell

anyone our little *secret*."

"I appreciate that."

"Really?" Scotty's voice rose in a manner I imagined the lump between his legs had. "How about you show me how much you appreciate my silence, Noah, with a kiss before our next classes?"

Having heard enough, I stomped into to my office, where I slammed the door and numbed my brain on social media, not feeling very social.

Martin called a special department meeting for later that day. The department conference room, across from Martin's office, had oak paneled walls surrounding an antique marble fireplace with the college logo proudly displayed on its mantel. The department's full-time faculty members sat at a long, polished, oak table looking like accountants before a market crash. At the other side of the room, under a large stained-glass window, stood the sacred snack table laden with coffee, tea, cookies, and fruit.

Between the two tables sat Wally Wanker on an overstuffed red armchair. At over ninety years old, Wally, between napping and waking, strained to hear and see what was going on around him. Wally had taught Voice and Diction in our department and was department head for many years. After he retired and moved on to Emeritus faculty status, Martin became department head and hired Millie Rodriguez to teach Voice and Diction. Since Wally has no life outside of the department, he spends most of his days in the department conference room reading, sleeping, stealing office supplies, or trying to engage anyone in conversation within earshot, like a Venus fly trap scoping out flies. While the rest of us generally wear casual dress clothing, Wally continues to wear the same worn gray three-piece suit he wore when giving mind numbing, incomprehensible lectures read from frayed, yellowed papers on the history of rhetoric before finally and thankfully retiring. Nearly every sentence out of Wally's ancient mouth starts with, "When I was department head...," which lands each time like a thorn in Martin's side.

At the conference table, starting at the head of the table and moving clockwise, sat Martin with Shayla, our department office assistant, sitting next to him. Shayla is African American, middle aged, smart, feisty, and takes her job seriously as Martin's sentinel.

Next sat Loptu Lee, our Playwriting professor. Asian American, of average height and weight, Loptu's black triangular-shaped hair infused with grey roots gave her a Cruella De Vil aura in reverse. This eerie look was heightened by Loptu's verbal outbursts due to her split personality.

To the left of Loptu sat Jackson Grier, our Movement and Stage Combat professor. Jackson is African American, tall, rail thin, and androgynous looking a la Ru Paul.

Following Jackson was Ariella Samson, our Costume Design professor, and David's widow. With long dark hair, sallow cheeks, and skin-tight, gothic clothing, Ariella gave Morticia Adams a run for her money.

Next sat Tyler Thompson, David's graduate assistant in Technical Theatre and the Technical Director/savior of my show.

Millie Rodriguez, teaching Voice and Diction, was next. A once beautiful Latina, at present Millie's wide hips, wilting hair, droopy eyes, and sunken cheeks gave her the appearance of a hound dog in a concentration camp.

To Millie's left was my graduate assistant in Directing, Scotty Bruno, who with cell phone in hand was admiring a selfie of him and Noah taken in Noah's office earlier. *Anyone up for another murder?*

Following Scotty, and sitting a bit too close to him for my liking, was Noah Oliver, our Acting professor and my personal heartthrob.

Sitting with Noah on my right and Martin on my left, I couldn't help thinking how different the department meetings will be sans David Samson. Generally, Martin starts the meetings asking if any of us have requested corrections to Shayla's draft minutes from the previous meeting. David immediately runs down his litany of corrections, which are thinly veiled attacks on what each of us had said at the previous meeting. When Martin begins the Old Business section of the meetings, David tells each of us what we have done wrong in our classes and productions that month. Moving on to New Business, David mocks and votes against any new curriculum or other proposal offered by any of us. At Committee Reports, David informs us that the committees upon which we serve are bureaucratic wastelands of inertia, and that we should stop insulting him with our senseless minutia.

Starting the meeting, Martin adjusted his bowtie and sweater vest (emerald today), thanked us all for coming, and called for a moment of silence in honor of David's death. Scotty whispered something in Noah's ear and they shared a giggle. Shayla shot silencing eyes at them and they froze like a stream in February.

What is the connection between Noah and Scotty?

During the meetings everyone at some point walks to the snack table to get something to eat or drink. Noah is usually kind enough to pour Wally his coffee. *I better listen to Martin…or face the wrath of Shayla, which means no computer service, office supplies, or snacks for a month!*

"I am sure that I speak for all of us when I say how saddened I am by the passing of one of our esteemed colleagues."

Unfortunately, Martin taught Theatre Management and not Acting. I don't think Mother Theresa would have believed his performance.

"David was a brilliant scenic designer, loving husband, and concerned colleague," continued Martin, somehow keeping a straight face.

Well, one out of three isn't bad.

Martin tried his best to summon up a pained look toward Ariella, who appeared anything but the grieving widow. "Ariella, our heartfelt condolences go to you and to your family."

Sitting on his armchair and watching the festivities, Wally's chin raised up from his knees, as he said, "When I was department head, David and Ariella were a couple. Now they're separated."

Ariella looked up from texting on her phone. "Thank you, Martin...and Wally. It helps me to jump back into my work."

Wally continued, "When I was department head I worked every day, sick or well. Shayla can tell you."

From my seat next to Martin's, I saw Shayla write on her minutes notepad to Martin, 'Yes, Wally was here every day. And he was one sick puppy!'

Martin smiled at Shayla's note, shot Wally a quieting glance then continued running the meeting. "Ariella, please let us know if there is anything that we can do to help you during this difficult time."

How about all of us joining together for a resounding chorus of 'Ding dong the creep is dead'?

Martin continued his speech like a president at a military funeral. "The funeral information will be emailed college-wide and posted in the local newspaper."

Wally responded, "When I was department head, David was a crook, a blackmailer, and a liar."

Ariella gave Wally a threatening glare.

Oblivious, Wally added, "When I was department head, I could never figure out why so many women preferred David to me."

'Let me make a list of a few hundred reasons,' Shayla wrote on her notepad.

Martin continued. "As most of you know by now, the police have been investigating this heinous crime, speaking to our students, staff, and faculty in the department. I know that you will each cooperate with their investigation to the fullest.

Detective Dickerson won't get my FULL cooperation.

Martin checked the notes in front of him then continued. "Detective Manuello also asked me to impress upon each of you the importance of not speaking to any member of the press."

Scotty kidded. "Even if the reporter is hot?"

After Martin shot Scotty a stifling glance, I noticed Shayla write on her notepaper to Martin, 'Where's a stage knife when you need one?'

Martin smiled at the note from Shayla then continued his announcements. "Scotty and Tyler will be taking David's classes for the rest of the term."

Scotty smiled like a politician at a corporate fundraiser.

Spraying coffee from his teeth, Wally said, "When I was department head I used adjunct instructors."

Scotty gave Wally the evil eye.

Martin responded, "We are fortunate enough to have two talented and competent graduate assistants in our department. Our students will continue to get the high quality education they have always gotten at Treemeadow."

To my dismay, Scotty whispered something to Noah who blushed.

Martin took a sip of his hot cocoa and continued. "As David's graduate assistant, Tyler will also take over for David on the college's Grants Committee and as advisor of the Christian Fellowship Club on campus."

Tyler stopped reading his stage lighting magazine and nodded to our leader.

"Any of David's students who are troubled or upset by this terrible incident can see our college's therapist or the Chaplin," explained Martin.

To do what? Count their blessings?

Millie softly whimpered, which eventually built into full blown sobs.

Loptu glared at Millie like a pit bull bitten by a poodle. "Save the theatrics for the stage, Millie."

Millie cried louder. Ariella groaned and continued texting her son.

Our department head tried to ease the situation. "Let's all be patient with one another. All of our nerves are frazzled due to this unfortunate situation."

Loptu was fit to be tied. She pointed to Millie and shouted, "The most *unfortunate situation* is that David fell for *her*!"

Millie responded with tears running down her face. "A man has died. How can you be so heartless, Loptu!"

Wally butted in. "When I was department head if a jilted lover attacked a current squeeze, I gave one of them a sabbatical."

Our department head took in a few deep breaths, as if trying to lower his blood pressure.

Loptu continued her rant. "Nobody's falling for your self-pity routine, Millie. So you can save the tears for cutting onions."

Shayla wrote to Martin, 'Somebody opened the cuckoo jar.'

Martin said, "Loptu, please, control yourself. This is a business meeting, and one of our colleagues has just been murdered."

Realizing that Martin meant business, Loptu opened her purse and swallowed a blue pill (prescribed for her split personality). Moments later she offered Millie a warm smile, "I really like your blouse. Where'd you get it?"

"It was a gift from David!" Millie burst out of the room, ran sobbing down the hallway, and slammed her office door.

Shayla wrote on her pad to Martin, 'And then there were nine.'

Jackson Grier lifted a long, thin finger. Martin nodded in Jackson's direction, and Jackson said, "I agree with Loptu. The first time. Why pretend we are upset over what happened to David? Why be hypocrites? I'm sorry Ariella, but I'll admit it. David Samson treated each one of us like dirt. I couldn't stand the swine, and I say he got what was coming to him."

Wally let out an asthmatic guffaw. "When I was department head I would have never hired someone like *you*."

Jackson glared at Wally. "Shut up, you old fool!"

Echoing Jackson and eyeing him at the same time, Scotty shouted at Wally, "Yeah, shut up, you old fool!"

Before Martin could intervene, Ariella moved her long dark hair away from her eyes, and said calmly, "You'll get no argument from me about David's behavior as of late, Jackson."

"May I Martin?" Martin nodded, and Noah continued. "The real issue here is that someone, one of our colleagues in our department, has been murdered. I don't think any of us will rest until the culprit has been found and apprehended."

Martin nodded. "Good point. We all need to be on our guard every minute to protect our students...and ourselves. The college has stationed extra security guards in and around our two buildings."

Wally dribbled his coffee onto his lap. "When I was department head we had our own security guard for this department."

Who was it, Hercules?

Shayla wrote on her pad, 'Would it follow meeting protocol if I throw Wally out the window?'

Martin wrote next to it, 'I listed that on the agenda under Fun and Games,' then he said, "Nicky, I am sorry to tell you that the play is being postponed for one week."

"Why?" Tyler looked like he was going to cry.

"Tyler, I know how devoted you, Jackson, Ariella, and of course Nicky are to this wonderful production, but the police believe this postponement is in the best interest of their investigation, and of our college. The college President agrees." Martin rearranged his notes. "Now, are there any other questions or comments about this issue?"

Shayla wrote to Martin, 'If anyone raises a hand, I'm going to start slitting vocal cords with my nail file.' Martin stifled a chuckle.

I was surprised that Wally didn't offer some words of wisdom about how he handled murder when he was department head.

Martin looked relieved to see no hands raised, and to see Loptu pop an orange pill into her mouth then sweetly compliment Jackson's scarf. "All right, let's move on to other business," said our department head.

Faster than you could say, 'when I was department head,' Wally Wanker toppled off his chair and landed at Noah's feet. Noah quickly felt Wally's throat for a pulse and couldn't find one. Wally Wanker had been wacked off!

CHAPTER THREE

I woke with a gasp like a sleep apnea patient, and realized I was in my office at the college. It was the next morning. I had been sitting at my office computer searching for clips of plays on tape to show to my Theatre History students and I must have dozed off. I had gotten very little sleep the night before since after my brush-up play rehearsal, I lay in bed as my mind jumped from question to question about the two deaths in my department. As if to ward off the evil spirits, I reached into my desk drawer, yanked out a handful of vitamins, and swallowed them with a chaser of apple juice leftover from my uneaten breakfast.

In an effort to make myself feel better, I visited Noah's Acting III class and stood at the back of the lab theatre. After each scene performance, I marveled at Noah's skill as he gave each student a sensitive yet on the mark critique for improvement, reminding the students to use sense memory, emotional recall, and listening and reacting for more believable characterizations.

I also noticed that the leads of my play were in their usual clique whispering like a U.N. committee before a war. This time Ricky appeared concerned about something and Paul, pecs protruding, seemed to be calming him down. As I unobtrusively walked by, I observed Paul rest his strong hand on Ricky's knee and gently coax it up Ricky's leg as Paul said to the group, "I'll talk to Kyle and make sure we get what's coming to us."

After Noah dismissed the class, noticing me in the back of the room, he made his way over to me. Noah looked as if he

39

had gotten even less sleep than I did. *Hopefully it wasn't because my graduate assistant snores.*

He said with a handsome smile, "Checking up on me, Nicky? I hope you haven't changed your vote for my tenure."

"You're a terrific acting teacher, Noah." I meant it.

Noah responded, "I don't feel so terrific. I can't get out of my mind the vision of Wally Wanker practically dying in my arms!"

"I know. Underneath all that complaining, Wally was a lonely human being with nowhere else to go but *here*, and nobody else to talk to but *us*."

With the students all gone, Noah yawned then put his head on my shoulder. "I'm so tired. I have the feeling that when the lights go out in the lab theatre for my next class, I'll join them."

I rubbed Noah's wide, smooth shoulders. Luckily I was standing behind him, so he couldn't see the baseball bat growing inside my pants. When I finished, I asked, "Better?"

Facing me, Noah nodded. Our eyes met, and we instinctively moved toward one another. I ran my fingers through his curly blond hair and he smiled. Not sure if I was coming on to Noah, Noah was coming on to me, or if the entire incident was the result of my exhausted imagination, I leaned into Noah with our lips just inches apart.

"Hello, detectives."

After Noah's half-hearted welcome, Detective Manuello and Detective Dickerson entered and stood grimly by the lab theatre door. Detective Manuello spoke first. "Good, you are both together."

I was pleased to see that Detective Manuello agreed that Noah and I would make a nice couple.

Detective Dickerson looked me up and down like a priest meeting a new altar boy. "We hope you don't mind, but we have a few more questions for you both."

Glaring at Noah, Manuello added, "We want to know why the evening cleaning staff believe *you* were the last person to see Professor Samson before he was murdered. We'd also like to know why the knife found in Samson' back had *your* fingerprints on it."

Coming to Noah's defense, I responded, "David was alive when Noah left his office, and many people handled that knife, including me!"

"*And*, Professor Oliver," Manuello continued, "we'd like to know why the coffee the other faculty members saw *you* give Professor Emeritus Wanker was the last thing Wanker drank before keeling over from ingesting large amounts of warfarin and coumatetralyl?"

Dickerson noticed the confused look on our faces, and explained, "Rat poison. Just like in that terrific Agatha Christie play you directed at the college a couple of years ago, Professor Abbondanza."

As I shifted my groin away from Dickerson's growing molars, Manuello explained, "The autopsy showed Wanker died from internal bleeding due to the poison in his system."

As if guest starring on a crime drama television program, Noah raised his arms in the air, and said, "I am not saying another word until I speak to a lawyer!"

"Bravo!" I shouted in support.

Detective Dickerson looked as excited as a plastic surgeon meeting a forty-year-old starlet. "This reminds me of that fabulous legal thriller play you did a few years back, Professor Abbondanza. I was completely fooled when—"

After shooting Dickerson a look that could melt the polar ice cap, Manuello said, "Professors, I advise you to think very carefully about what you are doing." Manuello looked like a starving python facing a suicidal lizard. "We could arrest you both as suspected perpetrator and accessory to the crime and continue our questioning at police headquarters."

Holding on to the back of a theatre seat for support, I responded, "You haven't built a solid enough case against Professor Oliver, or you would have already done that."

Manuello looked at me like Emperor Nero facing a peasant wearing a fireproof vest. "We may be issuing that warrant sooner than you think." Slowly moving toward the door,

Manuello said, "I look forward to seeing both of you gentlemen again."

The detectives were gone.

Well they spoiled that moment. After taking a few much-needed deep breaths, Noah and I walked down the hallway toward our offices. Hearing shouting coming from Jackson Grier's office, I stopped Noah and we stood outside our Movement and Stage Combat professor's door.

"Of course I appreciate what you did for me all those years ago, and what you did more recently. That's all the more reason I want to stop you from making a fool of yourself and destroying your life…and mine!"

Jackson sounded like a televangelist losing his tax-exempt status. Noah and I looked at one another then moved closer to the closed door.

"Yes, I love you, and I know you love me, but that doesn't give you license to act like a lunatic!"

"I wonder who he's talking to," I whispered to Noah.

Noah whispered back, "I bet it has something to do with what Jackson and David were arguing about."

At that moment Jackson whipped his office door open. Thinking of the deadly combat moves Jackson choreographed for my play, I thought fast and pulled Noah close to me for a long, amorous kiss.

Holding his office phone against his chest, Jackson said, "Can you two go find a room?" Then he shut his office door.

Before Noah and I could recover (from the threat of Jackson, and from our kiss), two reporters from the local newspaper surrounded Noah, looking like hikers spotting a tick.

"Professor Oliver, is it true that Professor Samson did not support your tenure, so you stabbed him?

"Did you poison Professor Emeritus Wanker when he refused to stop talking at a Theatre Department meeting?"

Protecting the man of my dreams, I said, "Professor Oliver is completely innocent, as you will find out very shortly. Now go back to your newspaper and make up some news."

Once shoulder to shoulder with our backs resting against the inside of my office door, I turned to face Noah with my mouth inches away from his. Thinking we might take up where we left off in front of Jackson's office, to my surprise, Noah said, "I think we better talk to Martin."

A few minutes later, Noah and I were once again seated in our department head's office, sipping hot cocoa on tall, leather wingback chairs next to the roaring fireplace. From my seat I could see Shayla, our department office assistant, perched next to the crack in the doorway to ensure she wouldn't miss a syllable of what we said.

After filling in Martin on our run-in with the detectives, I said, "It makes no sense. David is the rat. He's the one who should have been killed with rat poisoning."

As usual, Martin took control of the situation. "Noah, do you know why your fingerprints were found on the real knife that killed David?"

Resting his head in his hands, Noah answered, "Scotty gave me the real knife after the play's tech dress run-through two nights ago."

I did a spit take with my cocoa. "Scotty! *My* graduate assistant? *My* play's Assistant Director?"

Noah nodded and his fetching curls danced around his handsome face. "While Nicky was giving notes to the students, Scotty found me in back of the theatre. He asked me to bring the knife to David and ask if David could make it shine more brightly before opening."

So THAT'S what Scotty gave Noah in the box! I rubbed my forehead, hoping it would help my brain to function. "Why didn't you ask Tyler to polish the knife? He's the Technical Director for the show."

Noah shrugged his huggable shoulders. "Scotty asked me to bring it to David as Scenic Designer. I was on my way to David's office anyway — to ask David if he would consider supporting me for tenure."

A deep wrinkle grew across Martin's large forehead. "Noah, if you were on your way to see David in his office, what were you doing in the theatre next door?"

Noah snuck a warm look in my direction. "I was hoping for some moral support from Nicky before I encountered David. But Nicky was busy in the theatre giving notes, and I ran into Scotty." Noah turned to face Martin. "When I first arrived in David's office, I took the knife out of the box, put it on David's desk, and gave him Scotty's message. After David and I...had words, I left his office and went to find Nicky in the theatre lobby after he was finished giving his notes."

Martin adjusted his bowtie and sweater vest (canary today) and folded the canary cloth monogrammed napkin on his lap. "And that was *after* David told you that he would not support your tenure application."

"But David was alive after I left his office!" said Noah like an inmate on death row.

Closing his eyes in an effort to put together the pieces of the very puzzling puzzle, Martin asked Noah, "Why did you get Wally his coffee before the department meeting yesterday?"

I answered for my intended. "Because Wally is about a million years old. Noah was playing good Samaritan."

Noah was building up to near panic, "And I didn't put rat poison in Wally's coffee!"

Martin opened his eyes and looked at Noah like the prodigal son. "I know you would never harm anyone. And I certainly am not dissuading you from contacting a lawyer. But do you think it was a good idea not to cooperate with the police on this?"

Noah's cheeks turned scarlet. "What's the point in talking to him? Manuello has already decided that I murdered David *and* Wally. His investigation appears to start *and end* with *me*!"

"I agree with Noah, Martin."

Martin sat at the edge of his chair. "Many people despised David, and also found Wally as annoying as a stink bug...including me. *Anyone* could have come to David's office after you left and used that knife on him." He patted Noah on the knee. "And with each of us walking back and forth from the conference table to the snack table at some point during yesterday's department meeting, *any* of us could have poisoned Wally's coffee. *Each* of us had access to rat poison, since everyone in the department knows we keep a huge box of it in the Scene Shop to rid it, and the backstage area, of mice." Martin tented his fingers. "Since Detective Manuello doesn't seem to be doing it with an open mind, why don't *you both* investigate the crimes?"

As I envisioned questioning suspects shoulder to shoulder with Noah, I placed a theatre management magazine over my lap. "Are you suggesting that I play Holmes and Noah plays Watson?" *I always suspected they were lovers.*

"That is *exactly* what I am suggesting." His eyes twinkled. "As long as you tell me *everything* you find out."

My heart leapt in anticipation of spending more time with Noah. "It sounds like the game is afoot."

Noah took my hand. "Thank you for helping me. I will never forget this."

Our eyes met and our lips grew closer.

Martin spoke and I remembered he was in the room. "I volunteer to be your first interview, boys."

I laughed. "We know that you would never harm anyone in the department."

Raising his small palms, Martin responded, "*None* of us is above suspicion. With David gone, I am running for reelection as department head unopposed. With Wally deceased, I never have to hear, 'When I was department head' again." He sat back in his chair. "So, fire away."

I had directed a Sherlock Holmes play at the college a few years back. Sitting back in my chair and concentrating on the fire, I asked myself what Holmes would do (besides ravish Watson). I came up with my first question. "After Noah and I left your office two nights ago, you said you were going to talk to David about his latest shenanigans concerning Noah's tenure."

Martin nodded. "Correct."

"Did you?" Noah reached for a pad and pen to record

Martin's answers a la Watson.

"I started to," Martin explained, "but I realized it was after midnight. I was exhausted and not up for a verbal battle with David. So I decided instead to go home, get some rest, and confront David the following morning. Obviously that turned out not to be possible."

"Did anyone see you leave your office that night?"

Martin shook his head. "Everyone else had gone home, except for the cleaning crew. And they were no doubt hidden in someone's office with the Security guard, watching porn on a computer as usual."

"Did you see anyone go in or out of David's office?" I asked.

"I'm afraid not."

Watson changed the line of questioning. "Did you get up during the department meeting yesterday to get a drink or a snack?"

"No. Shayla placed my cocoa and apple at my place at the head of the table as usual."

I added, "Did you see anyone linger over Wally, or anyone try to slip anything into Wally's cup during the meeting?"

Martin laughed. "I was too busy reading Shayla's funny notes on her minutes pad."

"Well, Watson, it seems like we came up empty on our first interview." I turned to Martin. "I hope Holmes and Watson don't close on opening night."

"Nicky, you're a theatre director. Think about how you analyze a play before directing it." He turned to Noah. "Consider the characters, what are they doing, what do they hope to get, and what or who is in the way of them getting what they want?" Walking us to the door, Martin put his arms around us. "Talk to people. *Listen* to them. Notice what they are *and aren't* saying. Uncover the true meaning behind their words and actions." He squeezed my shoulder. "And don't forget to give me *all* the details."

As Martin opened the door to his office, Shayla nearly fell through the doorway, and said in a fluster, "Hello, gentlemen. I was fixing the knob on that old door."

It occurred to me that Martin had his match in an office assistant.

As Noah and I walked to our classes, I was happy to note that our visit with Martin appeared to have calmed him down somewhat. I was even happier when Noah asked me out to dinner with him that evening to discuss our investigation.

Before I left the house, I had tried on three different shirts and settled on my favorite purple button-down with tight, but breathable, black slacks and blazer. Noah looked adorable, as usual, in a turquoise button-down shirt, grey slacks, and white sweater. Sitting across from Noah, I picked up my menu and couldn't help salivating. Not over the menu items, but at Noah's blond curly locks bouncing on his smooth neck like foamy waves on the white sand. We were seated in a corner table next to a grey stone fireplace with nautical items encased in sea netting dangling over us. As we sipped our hot apple ciders (keeping our heads clear for the discussion ahead), I looked up at an antique ship's wheel and steered the conversation to us.

Noticing the candlelight illuminating his clear blue eyes, I said, "You look terrific tonight."

His smile was infectious. "So do you."

"It's nice to spend some time away from the college."

"It sure is."

We gazed into one another's eyes as Noah said, "We have to figure this thing out, Nicky."

That's exactly what I'm hoping.

Noah took out his notes. "Did you notice how apathetic Ariella appeared about David's murder at our department meeting?"

I put down my menu and begrudgingly shifted to Sherlock mode. "On the night of David's murder, David laid into Ariella in the theatre, critiquing her costumes. After David left for his office, while I was giving notes to the students, Ariella was backstage gathering costumes. After you left David's office, she could have gone to the next building and stabbed David with the knife. But why would Ariella poison Wally?"

"At the department meeting Wally mentioned that David dumped Loptu for Millie."

"So?"

"So, what if that was the first time Ariella had heard about it?"

"You mean Ariella literally killed the messenger?" I asked.

Noah sat back in his chair with a long exhale. "But unfortunately, like the knife in David's office, Wally's cup has *my* fingerprints on it."

"Elementary, my dear Watson!" *Okay, I'm overdoing the Sherlock Holmes thing.* "I did a bit of online investigating on rat poisoning and found that it takes *five to twelve hours* for a large dose of rat poison to kill a human being. So even with Wally's advanced age and failing health, the coffee you gave him at the start of the department meeting could not have killed him!"

"That's the best news I've heard in months!" He took my hand. "Thank you for researching that. You'll never know what it means to me!"

I'd like to find out.

After we ordered, I made goo-goo eyes at Noah over our crab cake appetizers, and he smiled giddily at me over our green salads. After our main course was served, sea bass for Noah and halibut for me, it finally seemed like the evening was moving on to more intimate territory.

"I really like being out with you, Noah."

"You're the best, Nicky." Noah squeezed my hand then went back to his notes. "Loptu wasn't at the theatre that night."

Giving up on our *hot date*, I said, "Though she's nuttier than a bat in Transylvania."

"Let's move on to our androgynous Movement and Stage Combat professor."

"Well, we know that David and Jackson argued in David's office."

A spec of hope grew in Noah's gorgeous eyes. "And Jackson lashed out at Wally at the department meeting when Wally mentioned that he wouldn't have hired 'someone like Jackson.'"

Finishing my three-cheese potato au gratin (and planning my next gym routine), I said, "What was it again that you heard Jackson say in David's office?"

"Something about getting a 'fresh start.'"

I wiped a glob of cheese off my chin, hoping Noah didn't notice.

Dropping his shoulders, Noah said, "In any case Jackson went in to see David *before* I did. So David was still alive when he left David's office."

After we ordered dessert (fruit and granola minus the nuts for Noah, and deep dish apple pie and more gym dates for me), I said, "Let's not forget our super-efficient department office assistant and protector of all things Martin."

"Ah, Shayla!" Noah said. "David tried to take the department head position from Martin, and Wally's constant stories about the past annoyed the crap out of Martin. Shayla is Martin's guard dog, but I can't see Shayla killing only two of us in the department. If she had her way, I think she'd take us all out."

We shared a laugh.

"Besides, Nicky, Shayla never works nights. Like most office staff at the college, she flies out the door at five pm as if the building is on fire."

After finishing every morsel of my dessert, and a bit of Noah's, I scooped a bunch of vitamins out of my pocket and swallowed them with a water chaser. Then I reached for my credit card to pay the bill, and Noah said he would pay the next time. *I guess that means there will BE a next time!*

As we waited for the waiter to collect my card, I put the saving grace of my play production on the suspect hot seat. "David scolded Tyler in the theatre. During notes Tyler could have snuck off to murder David, resulting in Tyler taking David's classes, faculty committee, and student club."

Noah responded, "Scotty got some of David's classes, too." The hope faded in his handsome face. "But neither Tyler nor Scotty has anything against Wally. They hardly knew him."

It's now or never. "Noah, speaking of my graduate assistant, I don't mean to pry, but I can't help notice how you and Scotty seem to have some sort of…*connection.*"

The color drained from Noah's handsome face. "I hope you don't think any less of me."

I wanted to crawl inside the sea shell candle on our tabletop.

"I'm not very proud of this." Noah waited for the waiter to take my credit card then after a deep breath said, "Before I came to Treemeadow, I met Scotty at a bar…in New York City. He was a college student at the time. I was an actor slash graduate student. We talked, laughed, danced, shared some drinks." Noah stared at the foamy water motif on the tablecloth. "When the bar closed we went back to my apartment, and we shared…more than drinks." Noah's eyes pleaded. "Please don't judge me harshly. I would have never done anything with Scotty if I knew that one day I'd be a professor in the same department where Scotty is a graduate assistant!"

I realized that I hadn't breathed for a few minutes. I took in a gasp of air, and asked, "Have you and Scotty been together — ?"

"No! Never once since I've been at Treemeadow. Please believe me, Nicky. I wouldn't do that!"

Raising an eyebrow, I said, "It's obvious that Scotty is still attracted to you."

"It's obvious that Scotty is still attracted to *everybody.*"

Clenching the leg of the table for support, I asked, "Are you still attracted to *him*?"

Noah's eyes softened. "How could I be attracted to Scotty?"

Like a country western singer belting out a refrain of love and devotion, I answered, "I believe you, Noah."

"Thank you, Nicky." He hugged me, and I melted like a

televangelist's make-up under the studio lights.

I held him by the shoulders. "But I would be careful around Scotty. I don't think he has totally given up on your...*past*."

"Good advice."

As we walked to our cars, I stood in my long coat, low-draped scarf, and winter hat. Noah pulled up the collar of his coat, and said, "How about we start our investigation with Millie tonight? I told her I would drop off the new list of plays from our library."

"Isn't it rather late for visiting?" I asked looking at my watch.

Noah opened his car door. "Acting and Voice are similar subjects. Millie and I have gotten to know one another well as colleagues. Come on, follow me."

Millie's house wasn't exactly where I thought this date would end, but follow you I will.

A few minutes later Noah and I were seated on either side of Professor Millie Rodriguez in her breakfast nook with cold cups of instant coffee in front of us. With her elbows planted on the Formica table, Millie rested her nail-bitten hands in her tangled, graying hair, and looked up at us with sad, sunken eyes.

"Thanks for bringing over the new play list, Noah. I'll use it in my classes." Millie looked down at the coffee in embarrassment. "Sorry, this is all I have in the house. I don't get many visitors."

I remembered how youthful and attractive Millie once looked...before she got involved with David Samson.

Noah's compassionate heart appeared to be breaking. "Nicky and I also came to see how you are doing after...everything that has happened."

Millie stared out her kitchen window into the dark, cold night. "I still can't believe it." She blinked back a tear. "My parents would have killed me if they had known I was dating David."

I asked, "Why is that?"

She sneered as if sharing a sick joke with herself. "Why do you think? Maybe because David was married!"

Noah added, "David and Ariella were separated. And David and Loptu had broken up."

Millie responded with a gloomy snort. "Pappy and Mama might have gotten over all that. It's all the rest of it."

Noticing Millie's fragile state, I asked gently, "What else about David would have upset your parents?"

She looked at me for the first time and could no longer hold back her tears. "You all talk about what a terrible person David was. But none of you know the truth."

Noah held her trembling hand. "Please tell us what we don't know."

Blowing her nose on the napkin, Millie said, "You don't know how kind and gentle David was with me. How he held me in his arms at night and told me that everything would be all right. The way he kissed me, and how he made love to me like it was a religious experience."

I changed tactics. "Millie, do you have any idea who might have killed David?"

She rubbed her red, swollen eyes. "It could have been anyone. What is it they say about *a woman scorned*?" She laughed cheerlessly. "Not to mention David was blackmailing Jackson."

"About what?" Noah and I asked in unison.

She added with despondent melancholy, "It wasn't as if David needed the money."

My ears perked up. "What do you mean?"

"David had many…enterprises." Millie rose from the table and stood on shaky legs. "I'm tired. I better go up to bed."

Noah and I stood, and Noah blocked her path to the stairs. "We are trying to help protect everyone, so nobody else gets hurt. Look what happened to Wally. Any of us might be next!"

"Wally!" Millie laughed and cried at the same time. "That old gossip. I don't think even Wally knew everything David was up to."

Putting my hand on Millie's sagging shoulder, I made my final plea. "Millie, please tell us what you know!"

She shook my hand off of her shoulder. "Ask David's son. As they say, 'like father like son.' And be ready for a *big* surprise." As she walked up the stairs, she added, "You guys can let yourselves out."

Outside of Millie's house, after Noah thanked me for dinner, I invited him over to my house to discuss Millie's responses, and for a *nightcap*. He seemed tempted but ultimately declined, noting we both desperately needed to get some sleep. So I drove home frustrated and alone.

I live in a furnished Victorian house owned by the college that resembles the set for the movie, *Meet Me in St. Louis*. What it lacks in heating efficiency, it gains in quaintness and charm. My aging paradise includes a front parlor with sliding doors leading to a back parlor, a dining room with wainscoting leading to a large bay window, double doors opening to a wood-paneled library, an eat-in kitchen, and a circular four-season room. Up the flared oak staircase are my bedroom, a guest bedroom, my study, and a bathroom with a claw-foot tub. In total, the house boasts seven wallpaper patterns, four fireplaces, three window-seats, and two mice who I affectionately named Nicky and Noah.

I was in my bathroom preparing for bed when I heard a loud banging on my front door. I threw on my bathrobe and rushed down the stairs two at a time. When I opened the front door, I found Noah standing on my wrap-around porch. I said a silent prayer that he had missed me and wanted to spend the night. My fantasies quickly faded when I noticed the look of horror on his face. "Noah! What's wrong?"

"It's Millie. She's dead!"

Chapter Four

The Theatre Department's conference room had the aura of a kingdom under attack. The sun shined through the stained-glass window, casting an ominous blood-red glow over each of us. We sat around the conference table in our usual places with the seats generally taken by David, Wally, and Millie palpably vacant. With our department head and department office assistant at the head of the table as King and Queen (You can decide which is which), we were like chess pieces on a chess board, wondering who would be next to leave the game. That is: the game of life.

The night before, after I called Detective Manuello, Noah was so frazzled he forgot his disclaimer not to speak to Manuello without a lawyer present. Sitting in my kitchen with a glass of whiskey in front of him, Noah answered each of Manuello's questions. After our visit with Millie, Noah had returned to Millie's house to retrieve the scarf he had left in her breakfast nook, secretly hoping that with just the two of them present Millie might spill her guts about David's dirty doings. Millie spilled her guts all right: all over her backyard. After checking the pulse in her neck to make sure Millie was indeed dead, Noah somehow drove to my house in a near hysterical state.

Based on what Manuello had told us last night after his search of Millie's property, it seemed that after Noah and I left her house, Millie had let someone into her home, and into her bedroom. This person in turn pushed Millie off her balcony, and she landed in her backyard with a broken neck. None of the neighbors had seen or heard anything suspicious.

What bothered me about this latest piece of the puzzle was that Millie obviously knew her murderer, and that Noah again was the top suspect, given his fingerprints on Millie's neck.

Detective Manuello, looking like Hercule Poirot after eating a case of donuts, stood next to the empty snack table in the conference room. Through the large window behind him, I could see local newspaper and television reporters swarming like bees around an allergic victim.

"Thank you, Professor Anderson, for asking your colleagues to join us here so early in the morning."

Martin nodded to Manuello. Since Martin was sitting between Shayla and me as usual, I noticed Shayla write to him on her notepad, 'I wonder what was more traumatic for the faculty, hearing about the latest murder or having to get up for an eight o'clock department meeting?'

Rolling the stomach fat under his shirt like pastry dough, Manuello said, "And thank you all for coming."

My usually garrulous colleagues sat silently, looking like deer on the first day of hunting season. Under the table, Noah squeezed my hand so hard I heard bones cracking. I didn't mind.

Moving to the stone fireplace with the college's insignia on the mantel, Manuello said in a sober tone, "After we found Professor Rodriguez murdered in her backyard, my first instinct was to shut down the college, or at least close the Theatre Department. However, Professor Anderson convinced me to allow classes and activities to resume as scheduled…for now."

My graduate assistant unleashed his pearly white laminates. "Martin, who is taking Millie's classes, faculty committee, and student club?"

Down boy. The woman's body is barely cold.

As always, having thought everything through in advance, Martin responded, "Tyler will take all of David's classes, and Scotty will take all of Millie's classes. Since Tyler has David's committee and student club, Scotty will take

Millie's place on the Professional Development Committee, and as advisor of the Forensics Club."

Tyler looked up from reading a tract from the Christian Fellowship Club and nodded.

As if being crowned Miss Congeniality, Scotty flicked back his bleached blond hair, smiled broadly, and waved to Martin with a squeezed-out tear covering one of his blue contact lenses. "Thank you, Martin. It will be my honor to pitch in!" Then as if Noah was one of the beauty pageant judges, Scotty rubbed his leg against Noah's under the table. I was relieved to notice Noah move his legs toward the back of his own chair.

Each of our heads moved from side to side as Manuello paced the room. "We may be dealing with random coincidental killings, or with a serial killer. In either case, we will continue to investigate every aspect of each murder, as well as work with the college's Director of Security to place additional security guards in each of the two theatre buildings on campus."

Loptu, our Playwriting professor, asked the first question. "Detective, you said Millie was murdered at her home. Will you be sending security guards to each of our houses?"

Scotty rubbed his shoulder against Noah's. "Or maybe we can double up to ensure each other's protection."

Running her black painted nails through her black and white hair, and dressed in black and white clothing, Loptu looked like an actress in a 1940's film noir. "Since each of the victims is...or *was* a member of the faculty in this department, I'd rather sleep next to Jack the Ripper than any of you." She searched inside her purse. "My mother back in Japan was right. I should have studied karate to protect myself from this nest of vipers!" She popped an orange pill into her mouth and suddenly took on a sweet persona. "Though I cherish each one of you dearly."

Manuello responded, "We are unable to supply each of you with a security guard for your home, but please be assured that police officers will be patrolling the neighborhood regularly."

That makes me feel about as safe as a virgin at a frat party.

Ariella raised her hand. Manuello seemed to like what he saw.

Dressed in black, as usual, and resembling Vampira, Ariella looked over at Noah. "I'm sorry to say this Noah." Her long dark eyelashes fluttered in Manuello's direction. "I'm not comfortable with the fact that Noah has been at each of the murder sites."

I would defend Noah in any court, including the court of courtship. "David was alive when Noah left David's office." I rose dramatically like the star juror in my past production of *Twelve Angry Men*. "It took five to twelve hours for the rat poison to kill Wally. And if Noah had killed Millie, why would Noah have reported the crime?"

Ariella responded in her usual monotone, "Perhaps to throw the detectives off the scent."

Jackson banged his hands on the table. "Will you all please *stop*! You are behaving like children!" His eyes bounced out of his head like a clown doll. "No offense Ariella, but David was a monster whose past caught up with him. Wally had dementia. Millie was suffering from a nervous breakdown. Have any of you thought that their deaths could have been *self-inflicted*?"

All eyes shot at Manuello like gamma rays in a science fiction movie. Manuello rubbed his wide nose and responded as if talking to a child with brain damage. "Stabbing oneself in the back is *not* a possible method of suicide."

Pointing his long, delicate index finger at Manuello, Jackson countered with, "But poisoning oneself and throwing one's self off a balcony sound like suicide to me."

Taking his trench coat off the coat rack, Manuello said, "The positioning of Professor Rodriguez's fall indicated that she was *pushed*."

Martin adjusted his bowtie and sweater vest (turquoise today). "And Wally, as Emeritus faculty, was the only one in the department who never ventured to the backstage area of the theatre, where the rat poison is kept."

Shayla wrote on her pad, 'Odd since Wally was a big fat rat.'

Untwining his long hair from the gold chain around his neck, Tyler said, "Maybe we can form a Neighborhood Watch. Look out for one another and tell each other when we are doing something that could put us in harm's way."

Manuello put on his coat. "That's an excellent idea."

Shayla's pad read, 'Now that Tyler is teaching David's classes, thankfully he wears normal clothes that cover his awful tattoos.'

Jackson stood and moved to the door. "I have a nine o'clock class."

"Professor Grier." Detective Manuello looked him up and down, noticing Jackson's long, graceful legs and straight as a board posture. "It would be good if you could help look after your colleagues."

His small features hardened, as Jackson responded sarcastically, "Is that, *detective*, because I am African American and *obviously* must be from a rough neighborhood?"

Scotty put his manicured hand to his face. "That's racist! How horrible!"

Manuello looked as if Jackson and Scotty had given him a one two punch in his ample stomach. "Professor Grier, as the Movement and Stage Combat professor at the college, I assumed you could defend yourself, and might be willing to try to help protect your colleagues."

"Well, that would just make my day." Jackson started to leave the conference room in a huff.

Scotty rose to go after him.

"Just a minute." Jackson and Scotty froze at Martin's words.

Martin continued. "Detective Manuello and Detective Dickerson will continue their investigation. I hope that each of us will be as forthcoming and helpful as possible in memory of our deceased colleagues, for the good of our students, and for the good of our department. I will email you all of the funeral information as soon as it becomes available. In the meantime, please go about your days as usual, but please also be mindful of what is going on around you. As Tyler mentioned, you might be the one to hear or see something that could save a life."

Shayla wrote, 'And the life could be your own.'

And go about my day I did. The post lecture activity in my Directing I class was for the students to form groups of four and create five silent living pictures per group to tell a story. This exercise is intended as exploration and development of how directors use actors in a creative and expressive manner. Since the students were unsurprisingly discussing the murders on campus when I arrived for class, I asked for their living picture scenarios to be based on murder and mayhem. After the students checked their cell phones, complained about the cost of their tuition and how hard the assignment was, I prodded them along and they got to work. I noticed that Paul's group was huddled in a corner enthusiastically planning their presentation. *Or are they planning something else?* Paul passed his phone to Ricky, Jan, and Kayla who watched something on the monitor as they giggled and gawked. When I moved over to try to take a look, Paul instantly put the phone away.

As each group took the small stage of our lab theatre classroom, I watched their group tableaus thinking about each of the three murders on campus. In the first scenario, the leads of my play appropriately used their bodies as living pictures to enact a murder with three people (Ricky, Jan, and Kayla) as jealous lovers of the same man (Paul). *That reminds me of the David, Ariella, Loptu, Millie quadrangle.*

The second group's picture plotline unfolded with a character's demise due to ambitious co-workers. *A la our graduate assistants Scotty and Tyler.*

Another group led us through a story about someone murdered for knowing a secret about someone else. *David and Wally knew a secret about Jackson. Millie knew a secret about David and his son.*

The next group featured a murderer who disapproved of her victims, thereby ending their lives. *Our department office assistant seems to disapprove of most of us in the department, except for Martin.*

The response to someone being bullied was the cause of the next murders. *David bullied all of us on a daily basis.*

In the last group's presentation, the murderer was a writer committing murders in real life to help realistically write them as stories. *Loptu, our split personality Playwriting professor?*

P.J. Myers, coming to class late as usual, joined none of the groups and instead sat love-struck behind Jan. After my critique session and class dismissal, P.J. presented Jan with a gold necklace. Jan in turn thanked him, put on the necklace, and left class calling after Paul Amour.

During my office hour, as I sat at my desk listening to students complain about grades and/or give excuses as to why they hadn't been to my class, I thought about Noah. He really seemed to like being with me, and to look to me for guidance and even affection. I believe his fling with Scotty is in the past. So why doesn't Noah take the leap with me? Perhaps it's fear of impropriety over my vote for his tenure. It could be my age. Maybe it's stress over the murders? Or maybe he's just not as into me as I am into him?

"Professor, my um cousin had a kid, you know, so that's why I um have been late to class lately and stuff like that."

Why? Did you deliver her child?

P.J. Myers was the last student to spin his yarn in my office. At medium height with a chubby build, blond hair combed straight up as if his hair was caught in a light socket, and piercings on nearly every appendage of his body, P.J. looked worth his weight in gold (literally). Having gone through various illnesses for his parents, the death of his grandparents, and needed escorts to the airport for siblings, he was now up to cousins having babies. Like many of my students, P.J. speaks in up-talk, meaning he raises the pitch of his voice at the ends of statements, giving him the added handicap of sounding unsure of his excuses.

I popped a few vitamins into my mouth for renewed energy and swallowed them with bottled water. "P.J., congratulations to you, and to your cousin, but this doesn't change the fact that you have been late for nearly every class session in Directing I this semester, therefore not fully participated in class exercises and activities. You also haven't done a great deal of the assignments, including working on the midterm project: analyzing, casting, directing, and presenting a ten-minute play performance for the class. Part of the director's job is to be on time, and to insist that others involved in the production are as well."

Sitting next to my desk and resting his chubby arm on my roster, P.J. asked, "Professor, will this, you know, affect my final grade for the class?"

"I'm afraid so. The final grade breakdown is documented on the class syllabus, which you received the first day of class."

P.J. whined like a child whose favorite toy had been donated to charity. "That is so like *unfair*! I'm a um Film major, not like a Theatre major and stuff like that. I like took your um class to learn the history of um directing, you know. Like *nobody* um directs plays anymore!"

"*I* direct plays, and I teach Play Directing." I looked at the antique clock on the oak fireplace mantel in my office and thanked Father Time. "P.J., my office hour is up."

"But what about um my cousin? Don't you like even *care*?!"

I stood and gathered my books and folders. "I hope your cousin and her baby are happy and healthy, and that they get to where they need to go on time."

"Um, one other thing, Professor. I like have to um get an A in your class."

"And why is that?"

"Like to pull up my GPA, since my like grades in my um other classes are, you know, pretty low and stuff like that.

You should be um honored. I like come late to your class, but I um don't like go at *all* to my other classes."

I showed P.J. to the door. "At this point, it will be difficult for you to get a D in Directing I."

Dazed, sweet P.J. turned into Clarence Darrow. "Then I will have to report this to the Dean of Students."

Looking into his desperate eyes, I answered, "Report this to the Dean of Students, the Dean of Administration, the Dean of Faculty, and the Dean of the Arts. Report it to the Dean of Bathrooms if you like!"

Using emotional recall, as I had taught him in one of the few classes he had fully attended, P.J. unleashed a flow of tears. "Professor, my parents back in Texas kinda paid my um tuition. If I flunk out and stuff like that they will, you know, *kill* me!"

I responded, "I thought your parents were in a car crash here in Vermont last week."

P.J. thought fast. "They um could have been, you know, visiting me from Texas." Obviously caught in his own lie, P.J. nervously fiddled with his lip ring. "Professor, the um real reason I'm like late to your class is that I've like been spending my um time, and money, buying gifts for Jan from your play and stuff like that. I um can't stop like thinking about her." He fidgeted with the gold chain connecting the ring in his nose to the ring in his chin then said adoringly, "When I like wake up in the morning, when I um daydream during the day, in my like dreams at night, Jan is, you know, all I can think about!"

Remembering my first crush (on my gymnastics instructor when I was five years old—don't ask!) and my latest crush on Noah, I inquired, "How does Jan feel about you?"

He tugged at the gold chain under his eyelid. "Jan like takes my um gifts and says like, 'thank you.' Then she like goes right back, you know, staring at um Paul Amour, the like lead from your show." Moving on to play with the black button lodged inside his earlobe, P.J. added, "I like spent all the um money my parents like gave me for my um textbooks and, you know, school supplies and stuff like that on Jan. I like love her so much. What am I like going to um do?"

I grabbed him by the dog collar around his neck. "You are going to go to your next class on time, and so am I!"

After critiquing the one-act plays in my Directing II class, I, along with Noah, were once again seated on tall, leather wingback chairs, hot cocoa cups in hand, in our department head's office. As usual Shayla's chair was planted at the crack in the doorway for ample eavesdropping. The amber glow from the flames licking the logs in the fireplace illuminated the newly sprouted wrinkles on Martin's face, revealing how much the murders had taken their toll on him.

"How are Treemeadow's own Holmes and Watson doing with your investigation?"

Running his strong hand through his gorgeous gold locks, Noah said, "I don't know what got into me, going back to Millie's place to get my scarf last night."

Martin shooed away Noah's concerns. "Who can blame you in this weather?"

"Isn't Millie's family back in Cuba?" asked Noah, genuinely concerned.

"I believe so." Martin took a sip of cocoa from the china cup and adjusted the turquoise cloth napkin on his lap then his turquoise sweater vest.

I slid to the edge of my seat. "Why did Millie look so ragged and downtrodden over the last few weeks?"

Martin responded, "Millie swore me to secrecy, but now that she is...no longer with us, I don't see the point in not telling you. But please keep this information just between us. Agreed?"

"My lips are sealed," Noah and I said in unison.

To my surprise, Martin appeared not to enjoy spreading a piece of news about someone. "A week ago, Millie came to me very upset. She asked for a few days off, which of course I gave her."

Noah beat me to it. "Why did she want time off?"

Martin's face saddened. "Millie was pregnant...with

David's child."

"I'm thinking *Rosemary's Baby* here!"

Silencing me with his eyes, Martin continued. "At first Millie was ecstatic, until she told David. At his age, David didn't want another child."

I added, "Especially with Millie?"

Martin nodded. "Somehow David talked Millie into…terminating the pregnancy."

Noah's face turned scarlet. "That bastard!"

I concurred. "With Millie's Catholic upbringing, that must have been torture for her."

"I've never seen Millie so upset," said Martin, "except after David was murdered."

While Noah simmered down, I changed tactics with, "Millie mentioned something about David blackmailing Jackson. Do you know anything about that, Martin?"

Martin looked like a puppy locked in a cage. "I wish I could tell you both about it, but Jackson has sworn me to secrecy."

Respecting Martin's confidentiality agreement, Noah and I promised to keep Martin informed on our investigation, and about any personal tidbits we might pick up.

On our way out, Shayla looked over the top of her computer monitor, and said to Noah and me, "Are you two boys an item yet?"

We giggled like schoolboys caught necking in the library.

Shayla's phone rang. She shook her head, and added, "For a bunch of college professors, you people sure act like children." Then she picked up the phone. "Lonely Hearts Club… I mean Theatre Department." After an irritated pause, she said into the phone, "I'll be right there." Taking a large key ring from inside her top desk drawer, Shayla said, "Sometimes I feel like Nurse Ratched. If one more of you locks himself out of his office, I'm going to lock you all in the loony bin!"

As Shayla walked past us, Noah and I said in unison, "Bye, Shayla," and left.

Walking back to our offices, Noah smiled. "Shayla's a gem."

I replied, returning the smile. "She knows all things."

"And she has the *key* to all things." Stopping at Noah's office door, he fished for the key in his pocket. "Thank goodness I didn't lock myself out of my office."

"Her bluster is all a façade. Shayla cares about each of us in the department, which is really nice." Admiring his handsome face, I added, "Especially for those of us who are single."

"If Shayla has her way, none of us will be single for long," Noah said with a laugh.

We searched one another's faces. As our lips grew closer, Noah said, "Nicky!"

I gazed into his sparkling eyes. "Yes, Noah?"

"Shayla has the key to each of our offices."

Not exactly the most romantic of phrases. "Right."

"And David was blackmailing Jackson about something that may tie into the murders."

Even less romantic. "True."

"So where would David keep his secret information about Jackson?"

Sherlock Holmes was back. "Elementary, my dear Noah. In David's office."

"And who has the key to David's office?"

"Our feisty department office assistant!" Before Noah held a press conference to announce we had solved the crimes, I added, "But Shayla will never give us the key to David's office."

His eyes doubled in size. "So, we will have to be a little *creative.* We're thespians aren't we?"

As Noah led me down the hall, he explained his plan, which sounded just crazy enough to work. When we reached Martin's office, as instructed by Noah, I hid outside the door (with my eye in the keyhole) and Noah approached Shayla's desk. Having returned from her errand, with Martin teaching his class, Shayla was alone in the office.

"Back so soon?"

Noah sat on Shayla's desk and unleashed his baby blues. "I missed you."

"You're not that good an actor, Noah," Shayla said with a firm push of Noah's tush off her desk.

Sitting on the tiny chair next to her enormous desk, Noah said bleakly, "I'm not much good at anything lately."

Shayla turned off her computer monitor. "Tell Mama all about it."

After a dramatic sigh, Noah said, "What's wrong with me?"

"You have a few hours?"

"What is it about me that is so incredibly unappealing?"

Shayla smirked. "Yeah, just look at you. Tall, gorgeous, smart, a college professor. You really hit pay dirt."

Putting his head in his hands, Noah said, "Then why doesn't Nicky see that?"

She clapped her hands together jubilantly. "I knew it."

On cue, tears appeared in Noah's sad eyes. "Shayla, do you know how hard it is for me to see Nicky every day and not smother my face in his amazing chest, wrap his muscular arms around me, and kiss his beautiful face, long sideburns, and strong neck?"

Is he acting?

"As much as I adore him, Nicky looks at me like a...used condom!"

"I could have lived without that graphic."

"What am I going to do?" Noah wept openly on Shayla's shoulder. As she wrapped her arms around him and patted his back, Noah waved me into the room.

With Shayla stroking Noah's tangled curls, I crawled on all fours to Shayla's desk and opened the top drawer. Feeling around inside, I moved slippers, body lotion, aspirin, antacids, pictures, an umbrella, rice cakes, a tissue box, a radio, a sweater, mittens, a seat cushion, a candy bar, breath mints, cough drops, a make-up bag, a hairbrush, a hand mirror, lip gloss, hairspray, a manicure set, and tampons. *And*

Moses thought he had it rough parting the Red Sea. After flicking off a wad of gum and pushing away a dripping perfume nebulizer, I confiscated the massive key ring. After locating the key marked D. Samson, I slid it off the key ring, dropped the key in my pocket, and carefully placed the key ring back inside the drawer. As I began my crawl out of the office, Shayla heard the creaky floorboard under my knees and turned toward the drawer. I dove under the desk just in time to avert her eyes. Sensing something was awry, Shayla was about to look under her desk when Noah let out a harrowing wail.

"I don't think I can live without him. What am I going to do?"

"Now, now. Nicky's just as stubborn and stupid as you are. He'll come around, then heaven help all of us with you two necking at department meetings. As if you making eyes at one another isn't annoying enough."

By that time I was out of the office with Noah following as he shouted, "Thanks, Shayla! I feel so much better now! Nicky and I will name our first child after you!"

As Shayla shook her head, and said, "White guys," Noah and I giggled down the hallway and landed at David Samson's office door.

Resting my back against the door, I said, "You were terrific, Noah."

As if accepting an Oscar, Noah responded, "Oh, thank you, Nicky. It really wasn't that difficult."

Hopefully you used emotional recall.

"You did a great job getting the key."

"Which Shayla will no doubt soon notice is missing, so we better work fast."

Relieved that the detectives' yellow tape had been taken down, I used the key to open David's door. Once we stepped inside the office, I quickly shut the door and Noah turned on the lights. We both let out a groan of disappointment when we realized that Detective Manuello or Ariella had already cleaned out everything in the office except an empty desk, two chairs, a barren side table, and a bookcase full of old books.

With slumped (but still beautiful) shoulders, Noah dropped his head to his stomach. "I'm sorry, Nicky. What a wild goose chase for nothing!"

"Not for nothing, Noah." *Try saying that three times fast.* I raced over to the bookcase and pulled on a book. It didn't budge. "This is the bookcase David designed for my production of an Agatha Christie play at the college before you graced our hallowed halls."

"So?" Noah looked at the tall mahogany bookcase with fake book fronts lodged in the shelves.

"So, if you pull on *this* book cover, the book case magically opens!" As I tugged on a dusty blue book cover, the book case split in half, revealing an entrance portal.

"You're a genius!"

Before I could bask in Noah's praise, the office door opened. Faster than a top one percenter getting a tax break, Noah and I dove into the bookcase and closed it behind us.

Though happily unseen by the intruders, Noah and I quickly realized that the space inside the bookcase was dark, dusty, and tight. On the positive side, however, my chest (and groin) pressed against Noah's, and I could feel and hear his breath, among other things, rising up and down. As the hardness in his pants grew, my manhood throbbed and expanded as well. Though enjoying the feeling of warmth and closeness with Noah, I seriously feared I would explode out of the bookcase.

Sensing my near panic attack, Noah wrapped his arms around me, nuzzled his head to my neck, and whispered in my ear, "Why do I smell Shayla's perfume? Is she in here too?"

Before I could respond, I heard the voices of Detectives Manuello and Dickerson outside the bookcase.

"I told you I heard something in here, Manuello."

"Well, there's nobody in here now."

"Why was the light on?"

"You tell me, Dickerson. You know everything about theatre and the theatre department."

"Maybe a maintenance person was cleaning up and left it on."

"That sounds good to me. Let's go."

At that moment a spider web brushed against my prominent nose. Certain that I would sneeze, I envisioned my prison cell, hopefully with Noah as my roommate. As I opened my mouth to let it rip, Noah buried my face into his chest to stifle the sneeze, causing my already monumental erection to nearly split my pants. Just as the detectives shut off the light and closed the office door, I let out a sneeze that soaked Noah's shirt, which matched my soaked pants. This sent the detectives back into the office with a final search and a disgruntled declaration about "mice in these old buildings."

Once satisfied that the detectives had come (as evidently had I) and gone, I pulled a lever (not what you're thinking) inside the bookcase and Noah and I were free at last. Noah quickly exited and turned on the light. As I stepped out of the bookcase, I noticed a strong box at my feet. After announcing my find to Noah like a Bingo winner at a church social, I yanked the box out of the bookcase and onto the desk. Using my pen knife, I pried it open then rifled through its contents with Noah. After perusing various set design plans from David's past shows and love letters from David's numerous girlfriends, Noah and I were ready to declare our mission a failure, when a picture slipped out of one of the folders. It was a photograph of an attractive African American woman sitting at an office desk. Assuming she was one of David's past girlfriends, I was about to replace the picture inside the folder when something caught my attention.

"Noah, look at this picture."

Examining the photograph, Noah said, "She looks familiar. Who is she?"

I turned over the picture, and read the caption, "Dr. Jillson Grier, PHD."

"Does Jackson have a younger sister?"

"He never mentioned one."

"Maybe that's who he was talking to on the phone in his office?"

"I don't think so, Noah." As I stared at the picture, thinking about Jillson and Jackson, I suddenly realized why David Samson was blackmailing Jackson Grier.

CHAPTER FIVE

The beautiful, dark-skinned women lay on her chaise helplessly watching the red blood drip from her neck to the floor. As she clutched her ivory dressing gown and cried out for mercy, the handsome, masculine man standing over her smiled in delight. She summoned her last breath to ask, "Why?"

With dark eyes ablaze, he tossed back his long flowing mane of hair. "The Lord gives, and the Lord takes away." His sinister laugh permeated my consciousness.

A gorgeous, young, blonde woman entered my field of vision. Upon seeing the wounded woman lying helplessly, she screamed and clutched at her heaving breasts. Then she fervently accused the handsome man of all things vile. He took her in his arms, kissed her passionately, and she left the room as it faded to black.

"End of Act I. Let's take a half hour break then resume for Act II," I announced.

My student stage manager, SuCho, screamed, "Half hour break, everyone!"

As Paul and Kayla left the stage, I was sitting in my director's spot in the audience taking notes at yet another evening technical rehearsal. After our earlier bookcase escapade, Noah and I returned David's office key to Shayla during a second round of Noah crying, "Why doesn't he love me?" and Shayla threatening to make Noah pay her blouse cleaning bill.

"How did Act I go?" Tyler plopped himself down next to me and the familiar smell of pepperoni and sawdust filled the air.

"I love all of the colored lighting effects, and the projections of the streets and the river are amazing!"

"Thanks, Nicky." As Tyler ran off to dangle from the catwalk and refocus some lights, I thanked the theatre gods for such a diligent Technical Director.

As my Assistant Director took the vacated seat next to me, I noticed a worry line appear amidst the tan makeup on his forehead. "I'm concerned about something."

"What is it, Scotty?"

He sat back in his chair and flexed his abdominal muscles. "Since that overweight detective took our real knife, I'm concerned that the fake knife won't look macabre enough for the final scene of the show."

"It will have to do." I added, "Speaking of the real knife, I've been wondering why you gave Noah the real knife to bring to David that night?"

Scotty looked at me like a non-native speaker. "David was the Scenic Designer for the show. I asked him to polish it."

"But why didn't you ask Tyler to do it? He's the Technical Director?"

"You know Tyler. He's always hanging from somewhere fixing something. I couldn't find him."

"Agh!" Something landed on my lap. Unfortunately it wasn't Noah.

"Sorry, Nicky," said Jackson, as I handed him back the rubber knife. "I was going over the fight scene in Act II with Paul and Ricky and the prop got away from us."

Batting his eyelashes like Scarlett O'Hara at the cotillion, Scotty said, "The fight scene looks terrific."

Jackson squared his shoulders a la Rhett Butler. Then he threw the fake knife to our leading man.

Paul bent over to stretch his bulging calf muscles, and said between his legs, "I was pleased with it."

Translated, Paul was pleased with Paul.

Ricky was behind Paul faster than a train heading out of a burning tunnel. "Paul, can we like go over that last move again, where you um grab me by my waist and kinda hurl me over your shoulder?"

Jan appeared on Paul's other side. "Can we...um...run lines for our like love scene in, you know, Act II?"

Paul appeased his adoring fans, and the three students moved backstage to privately rehearse their scenes for Act II.

Standing between Scotty and Jackson, I felt like a kid with a fever blister at a spin-the-bottle party. "Jackson, can I speak with you a moment? Scotty, do you mind?"

After nearly devouring Jackson with his eyes, Scotty left Jackson and me sitting side by side in the theatre.

"Is there a problem, Nicky?"

"Yes, but not with the fight choreography. Why did you go to David's office on the night he was murdered?"

Jackson looked away. "I'd rather not say."

I took his soft, graceful hand in mine. "I know about Jillson."

His eyes dropped to his knees. "Does anyone else know, besides Noah of course?"

I shook my head then said softly, "Please tell me about it. Being gay and transgendered, we're both out of the same square box. You can trust me."

Seeming satisfied with my assurances, he looked around the theatre to make sure it was empty then turned back the pages of time. "Growing up in the South and being forced to wear dresses, play with dolls, and join girls' groups at school and at church nearly killed me. The only thing that kept me alive was knowing that I could get out of there someday and become what I...already was."

"A man."

He nodded. "My family wanted nothing to do with me or with my...decision. After paying for college myself, I worked as a college professor until I could save enough money for the psychiatric visits, hormone treatments, and ultimately the surgery. After that, I applied here under my new and finally *right* persona."

As department head Martin would do the reference check. "And you argued about your *fresh start* with David in his office that night?"

Tears filled Jackson's almond-shaped eyes. "That pig suspected something was *amiss* when he did his own background check on me prior to my coming to Treemeadow. David snooped further online and found what he was after."

I put my hand on Jackson's shoulder. "So what happened that night?"

"David had been blackmailing me for months. I wasn't...and I'm not ashamed of my past. It's just so much easier to start over without baggage, especially working with young people as we do."

I nodded. "So you and David argued?"

"*David* argued. I laid down the law that I was no longer going to give him any more money."

"And David didn't like that."

"You hit the tail on the bigot."

We paused while Tyler obliviously fixed a sconce on the wall of the theatre house.

Once Tyler hurried off to do his next chore, Jackson said, "David threatened that if I didn't continue to pay him, he would tell everyone, including the college's Board of Trustees, about my past. I told him he could go stick his threat where the sun don't shine, and I stormed out of his office."

"Did you come back to David's office later that night?"

He shook his head like a wet horse. "No way. I'd had enough of that cretin."

"When David was blackmailing you, he probably told Millie about it."

"That makes sense, since they were lovers."

"But how do you think Wally found out about it?"

Jackson raised his eyes until they became white clouds. "That old gossip probably searched Martin's records when Martin wasn't in his office."

Imagine snooping in a colleague's office! "To do that, Wally would have had to get past Shayla. That's like passing a pit bull that hasn't eaten in six months."

"Not if Wally did it at night when Martin and Shayla weren't there."

"Was Wally on campus at night?" I asked in surprise.

"Sure. That's when Wally filched office supplies."

"And Wally had the key to Martin's office?"

"He was department head before Martin. Wally never turned in his office key."

I rested my foot on the seat in front of me. "Jackson, who were you arguing with on the phone when Noah and I passed by your office? You were saying something about the past and future."

"Sorry, I don't remember, Nicky."

A group of students called for Jackson. After excusing himself, Jackson made a welcome retreat backstage.

I walked on stage to check the lights, sets, and props. It was no surprise to find Tyler sitting on the stage floor repairing a sound speaker. I worried that his long hair, gold cross chain, or thick, tattooed arms might get caught in the wiring and he would be electrocuted. My fears subsided when he replaced the speaker frame and pronounced the speaker ready to go for Act II.

"Tyler, how is it going teaching David's classes?"

"Not too much different from before."

"What do you mean?" I asked.

He explained. "David had me teaching his classes while he snuck off to meet Millie at her place or visit his son in the Film Department on campus." Tyler moved on to his next project, putting glow tape on the lip of each stair on the set so the actors wouldn't fall in the dark.

Following him, I asked, "And all is well advising the Christian Fellowship Club for David?"

He ripped off some tape. "They're a nice bunch of kids with their heads on straight."

I had advised the Pagan Club, the Stonewall Club, and now the Theatre Club, and it was always time well spent.

"Do you like taking David's place on the Grants Committee?"

Placing the tape at the edge of each step, he replied, "Sure, unlike David I'm not taking the money for myself. Obviously David didn't subscribe to, 'Thou shalt not steal.'"

We shared a laugh.

I kneeled next to him. "Tyler, did you spend any time with Millie?"

"I saw Millie a lot since she and David were so hot and heavy."

Another one of those sticky little commandments broken by David. "Did you ever go to Millie's house?"

Finished, he stood up. "Once or twice...to give her something from David."

"Like what?"

"David liked to give Millie gifts, and she liked receiving them."

No doubt paid for by the money David stole. "Did you ever get Wally anything to eat or drink?"

"Since I'm a graduate assistant, I've gotten all the professors something at one point or another, Nicky." He grinned, unveiling two adorable dimples. "Except for Noah. Scotty seems to take care of him."

Rub it in, Tyler.

After Tyler hurried off to replace a stage rope, I walked into the Costume Shop to approve the costumes for Act II. Taking in the scent of sweat, steam, and detergent; I found Ariella teaching a student how to repair the hem of one of Jan's silk dresses in the show. After completing her task, the student clutched her cell phone like it was a flask of vodka at a rehab clinic and rushed out of the shop. As Ariella ironed Paul's low V-neck shirt for Act II, Scene III, I sat on the cutting table and examined each costume.

"The costumes really bring out the menacing mood of the show, Ariella. You did an amazing job."

Clad in a skin-tight black sweater, long skirt, and shawl with her black hair in a bun, Ariella looked like a character in the play. "Thanks, Nicky. It's a great show."

I smiled. "Can I ask you a personal question?"

78

The lines in her face softened. "Now that I'm single, are you going to ask me out?"

After a laugh I asked, "Actually, I'm wondering why you married David."

Ariella hung up the shirt and moved on to replacing a button on Paul's skintight pants. "Believe it or not, when we first met, David was very sweet."

"I believe it. How did you two meet?"

"This is going to sound corny, but our parents introduced us."

"Was it love at first sight?"

"Pretty much." She smiled, which is rare for Ariella. "David was such a gentlemen. He always made sure I was comfortable, and that I felt happy."

I noticed a picture of David, Ariella, and their son on Ariella's desk. "And you two had a son together." Feeling like our department head, I asked, "What went wrong between you and David?"

Ariella hung up the pants. "David and I both grew up poor. It never bothered me." She shrugged her broad shoulders. "How could I miss what I never had?"

"But being poor bothered David?" I helped Ariella move the costumes for Act II from the Costume Shop to a moveable clothing rack near the Costume Shop's doorway.

"It was an obsession with David to gather wealth...to never be poor again. He thought about it every minute of every day. So the loving man I married became driven, angry, and obsessed with getting things that I never wanted in the first place."

Following Ariella as she wheeled the costume rack backstage, I asked, "Is that why David stole grant money from the college?"

She replied over her shoulder, "And look where it got him, Nicky."

We stifled our conversation while Ariella gave the student actors their costumes for Act II, Scene I, and they went to their dressing rooms to change (with Danny, Jan, and Kayla volunteering to assist Paul with his costume change).

Once Ariella and I were alone again, I asked, "Do you know why David broke things off with Loptu?"

"Probably because she's psychotic…like the plays she writes."

"Do you know why David and Millie were having problems?"

Ariella's shoulders dropped. "I took one look at Millie and knew she was pregnant. Millie was overjoyed. David wasn't. David told me what he wanted her to do. I went to Millie's house one night to try to talk her out of it. She wouldn't listen to me. She kept calling me the *jilted wife*. Before she threw me out, Millie told me something horrible about David and Kyle."

"Kyle?"

"Our son. He's a Film major here at Treemeadow."

Kyle! Didn't Paul mention something to Jan, Kayla, and Ricky about talking to Kyle? I touched her hand. It was ice cold. "What did Millie tell you?"

"David and Kyle both denied it."

"Denied what?"

She clutched at my hand. "It can't be true, Nicky. It just *can't*."

"Professor! Professor!" I looked behind me to find P.J. from my Directing I class cowering behind a teaser curtain.

Leaving Ariella, I stood over P.J., and used my stern teacher voice. "What are you doing at my *closed* technical dress rehearsal?"

He rose to his feet. "I like know I um shouldn't be here and stuff like that." Clearly struck by all of Cupid's arrows, he added giddily, "I was like hoping I could, you know, see Jan."

I calmed down at the sight of puppy love. "Jan is playing one of the leading roles in the show." Careful not to catch my hand on any of the gold jewelry dangling from his various facial piercings, I put my hand on P.J.'s shoulder. "Therefore, Jan can't entertain suitors right now."

"Oh, I don't like want to sell her a suit, Professor. I want to ask Jan if she'd like go out with me and stuff like that. She is so like incredibly um beautiful." His eyes bulged. "Oh, don't like think I'm just into Jan's packaging and stuff like that. I'm totally into the *whole* like package, you know, inside and outside."

I walked him out the backstage exit, down the hallway, and into to the theatre lobby. "P.J., I agree that Jan is beautiful, talented, and a nice student, but she is very busy right now."

Standing in his brown parka, leaning on a gold marble column, P.J. answered, "That's the like problem. Jan um is *always* busy! How can I um ever ask her out, you know, if I like don't ever um see her?"

Walking him to the lobby entrance doors, I said to Jan's gentlemen stalker, "All is fair in love and war, but *not* during tech rehearsal." I opened the door and gently pushed him out into the cold night air. "Get home safely, P.J. See you in class — on time." I shut the door behind me. Through the glass window, I watched P.J. walk with lowered head through the covered bridge.

Commiserating with P.J's unrequited love, I swallowed a handful of vitamins with a bottle of water and thought about Noah. Then tending to the stirring sensation in my groin (not what you're thinking), I ducked into the men's room. Once positioned at the urinal, I unzipped my pants and began to take care of business. Seconds later I heard the door open behind me and felt a presence at the next urinal.

"Holy cow!" Detective Dickerson had snuck a peek. "That's the biggest dick I've ever seen!"

I blushed. "I get that a lot."

"I'm not surprised!" Dickerson watched in fascination as I urinated.

I finished, zipped up, and flushed. "What are you doing here at night, Detective Dickerson?"

Retrieving his salivating jaw from the floor, the ginger-haired, blue-eyed detective finally made eye contact with me. "Detective Manuello and I are checking more tips."

"Have you come to any conclusions?" I asked.

"As you know, Manuello likes your friend Professor Oliver for the murders. I'm not so sure."

"Kudos to you."

He smiled revealing a handsome set of white teeth. "Can I ask if you and Professor Oliver are a…"

Dickerson was so closeted he couldn't even say the word.

"Noah and I are not lovers." *Yet.*

Dickerson flushed and joined me at the sink area to wash up. "Talking in the bathroom like this reminds me of that scene in your amazing production of that homosexual play."

Not letting him off the hook (no pun intended), I replied, "Detective, why did you ask me if Professor Oliver and I are lovers?"

He looked at our reflection in the mirror. "To be honest, I wondered if you were single."

"And why is that, detective?"

Having finished washing our hands, we both reached for the towel machine at the same time. Dickerson handed me a paper towel. "You're a great director. And you seem like a nice guy."

I stepped back. "I've read about cops coming on to gay guys in public wash rooms then arresting them for solicitation."

Dickerson wiped his hands. "That's not what I'm doing."

Reaching over him to throw away my towel, I asked, "Then what *are* you doing, detective?"

"Call me, John," he said with a twinkle in his eyes.

"What are you doing, detective?"

He moved in closer and I smelled his citrus cologne. "I thought maybe we could get dinner some time."

I backed away. "I'm sure your *wife* would like that."

Smiling, he replied with a seductive wink, "We have an *open* marriage."

"I'm sure it's open on *your* end, detective." *Very open.*

He leaned against the sink and his shoulders bulged under his blazer. "I'd like to be friends, Nicky."

"Sorry, I don't date married men."

He placed my hand on one of his biceps. "I'm betting you'll make an exception with me."

Removing my hand, I answered, "Don't bet too much, detective."

"Relax, Nicky. I won't tell anybody."

Before I could respond, Dickerson pressed his pelvis against mine, took my head in his strong hands, and kissed me hard on the mouth. Just as I was about to stick his head under the faucet, I heard the bathroom door open. I looked up to see Noah in a state of shock.

The heat rose up my face like a curtain at Tara.

Dickerson played the role of professional detective again. "Professor Oliver, your colleague, Professor Abbondanza, just came on to me."

I shrieked. "Noah, that's not—"

Noah raced out of the bathroom with a tear lodged in the corner of his eye.

"Noah, wait!"

Dickerson grabbed my arm. "Let him go." He put his hand on my crotch. "I want to get to know you better."

"Take a hike back into your closet, Dickerson."

I pushed Dickerson away and left the bathroom, rushing to catch up to Noah in the hallway. "I think you mis—"

"It's no secret that you are my closest colleague and friend at the college." Noah's gorgeous blond locks bounced as his beautiful sapphire eyes looked at me with melancholy. "So I can't stand by quietly while you hook up with someone like Detective Dickerson." Noah counted off on his beautiful fingers. "For one, he's married. Two, he's totally insincere. Three, he seems to want nothing more than your—"

"Dickerson came on to *me* in the bathroom. After you left, I told him in no uncertain terms that I'm not interested."

"But Dickerson said…and you two looked liked you were—"

"He lied. We weren't. I wasn't."

"You weren't?" He looked at me hopefully.

I shook my head so hard it nearly fell off my neck. "I'm not interested in Dickerson."

Holding back a tear, Noah said, "From the moment I first met you, I liked you." He looked down at the floor. "I *more* than liked you."

My heart did the Macarena.

"Don't freak out, Nicky. It's always disappointed me, but I accept that you don't want to be with me...in a romantic way. But please be careful of Dickerson. Regardless of your intentions, he could be setting you up for some crazy solicitation charge...or something worse!" Straightening his baby blue sweater, Noah said, "I have to finish grading papers. Please think about what I said."

I followed Noah into his office, and said regally, "Noah, I have done as you asked and thought about what you said. And I have come to the conclusion that I absolutely cannot be interested in Dickerson."

Noah looked at me with searching eyes. "Why is that?"

I put down the pen in his hand and lifted him off his chair. "Because how could I be interested in Dickerson when from the first moment I met you I have been totally nuts about *you*?"

"What?" Tears filled his welcoming eyes. "But, how come you never — ?"

"Because you are going for tenure. I didn't want you, or anyone in the department to think I was trying to coerce you into getting involved with me to win my vote."

Looking like he could be blown over with a feather, Noah said, "Nobody would have thought that!"

"How come you never came on to *me*?"

"Because I thought you weren't interested in me, and I didn't want to ruin our friendship."

I moved his face to meet mine. "Nutty boy, I am *totally* interested, and *totally* crazy about you."

As he stared at me in giddy disbelief, I put my arms around Noah's broad, smooth shoulders, gazed into his handsome face, and pressed my lips against his. We shared a warm and wonderful kiss. Noah took in a shocked burst of air then he kissed me back, deeper. As I kissed every inch of his stunning face, Noah bathed in the warmth of my breath and the love in each of my caresses. After kissing and hugging like two teenagers at a drive-in movie, we finally came up for air as SuCho shouted down the hallway, "Act II going up, Professor!"

Noah whispered in my ear, "Things are going up all right."

I nodded, "This is the beginning of a new act, starring you and me."

Chapter Six

The moment after I gave my last note at the technical dress rehearsal, Noah and I drove like drag racers (no pun intended) and parked in my frozen driveway. The second we hit my wrap-around porch, though it was only fifteen degrees outside, we began tearing off our clothes as if they were on fire, like us. Once inside, taking two steps at a time, we flew up the fanned oak staircase and finally reached my bedroom, wearing nothing but our socks. *It's winter!* I tackled Noah as if he was a tight end (which he is) and hung on to him like a lifesaver (which he is). Nestled in one another's arms in my white canopied bed, we kissed and blew sweet nothings into each other's ears.

I ran my fingers above, below, and through Noah's luxurious blond curls. Next, I tickled the soft, golden hair on his arms and legs. Then my tongue licked his nipples, abdominal muscles, and navel. When I took him inside my mouth, Noah moaned in ecstasy and begged for release. Instead I straddled his neck, dangling my genitals in front of his face. Noah looked up at me like a bankrupt jeweler facing the Hope Diamond. He flicked, kissed, licked, and to my surprise, greedily deep-throated all nine and a quarter inches.

I flipped him over onto his side and licked his wide, smooth back and caressed his firm buttocks, thigh, and calf muscles. When I could not hold back any longer, I suited up and entered him. We rocked back and forth as we kissed and caressed until we both shouted our orgasm, no doubt waking everyone on the block. As we spooned, we hung onto one another, vowing never to let go.

After showering, and massaging one another with my Luffah, we dressed then ate a huge dinner in my dining room. I commented on what a great co-chef Noah was as we devoured our poached salmon, root vegetable medley, and salad with warm goat cheese, walnuts, and beets — minus the walnuts for Noah. While eating our dessert, hot apple cobbler, we started to giggle.

"I can't believe it took us this long to get together," Noah said, while licking cinnamon off his palm.

I kissed his nose. "I didn't think you'd want an old coot like me."

"You're only seven years older than me."

"In gay years that's twenty-one years older."

"Okay, I'll call you Daddy," he said with a devilish look in his beautiful eyes.

I slapped his butt and he hugged my neck. Saving the dishes for the morning, we went through the dining room double doors across the long sconce-laden hallway to the back parlor, where we sprawled out on the Victorian style sofa next to a roaring fire. With my long legs wrapped around him, Noah's rested his head on my chest, and I stroked and kissed his forehead and hair. We stared at the dancing flames and thanked the cosmos for finding one another.

After sitting up and resting his shoulder on mine, Noah asked, "Should we tell everyone at the college that we're...*together*?"

My favorite new word. "Why not?"

"Do you think it might *complicate* things?"

"Noah, there have been three murders at the college. Our personal lives are the last thing anybody will care about."

As if suddenly remembering, Noah asked, "How did the investigation go today without me?"

A log crackled in the fire. "Bad news for you. Scotty seems taken with Jackson now."

Noah squeezed my hand.

I continued. "David found out that Jackson was Jillson via the internet and was blackmailing him."

Noah did a double-take and his hair flicked against my cheek. "*Blackmailing* him?"

I nodded. "We have to keep this just between us, Noah. Okay?"

"Ooow, I like the sound of that." Noah licked his lips.

I squeezed his nipple. "And Tyler and Ariella admitted they'd visited Millie at her house. Tyler on an errand with gifts from David, and Ariella to try to talk Millie out of caving in to David's wishes to have the abortion. So, they both knew where she lived."

Noah rested his back against my chest and wrapped my arms around him. "This is like a soap opera!"

I squeezed him closer. "And Ariella is worried that there may have been some dirty dealings going on with David and their son Kyle."

"Such as?"

"She doesn't know for sure, or rather she doesn't *want* to know."

Noah kissed my hand. "Well, you sure uncovered some good dirt without me."

I tickled his stomach. "But there's a lot more to do, Watson."

He laughed. "I like the sound of that, Sherlock."

"Me, too."

We giggled, kissed, and cuddled until sunrise.

* * *

The next morning, Noah and I shared a hot asparagus omelet and a hotter shower. After we kissed goodbye in my vestibule, Noah was all that I could think about for the rest of the day.

At the campus gym I told the student at the desk I was going to use the Noah instead of the Nautilus. At a faculty committee meeting I called the keynote speaker, the key Noah speaker. At lunchtime in the cafeteria, I asked for stir-fried veggies and *Noahs* instead noodles.

Finally after our classes were over, we met up in Noah's office, shut the door, and embraced as if I had just come home from the war. Sitting on the window seat in his office and sharing our days, we held hands and watched the snow fall outside like a white fluffy blanket on the campus lawn, covered bridge, gazebo, and Gothic buildings. As I looked out at the giant, bronze statues of Treemeadow's founders, Harold Tree and Jacob Meadow, I said, "Can you believe we teach at a college founded by a gay couple?"

He kissed my cheek. "I wonder if they were as happy as we are now?"

I looked at the statues' solemn expressions. "They don't look too happy."

After pointing out their three-piece suits, Noah added, "Maybe they looked happier when they were *out* of their clothes?"

"That must be it."

After we kissed, we decided that if anyone erects a statue to us, we will insist that we are kissing in bronze.

Our steamy solitude was interrupted when two local television news reporters pushed into Noah's office. They shined a light atop a television camera in our faces and lowered a boom microphone over us, as they asked accusingly, "Professor Oliver, did you and Professor Rodriguez have a lover's spat before you threw her off her balcony?" "Professor Abbondanza, was Professor Rodriguez threatening to out you before you silenced her permanently?"

As a consummate actor (meaning a ham), Noah faced the camera and turned on his charisma. "I would like to set the record straight for the viewers at home. I am not a murderer. Professor Abbondanza is not a murder. As difficult as it may be to comprehend when looking at them, I believe Detectives Manuello and Dickerson will eventually bring the murderer to justice...with some help from us."

Before Noah could put his entire leg in his mouth, I shooed the reporters out of Noah's office, shouting, "No comment."

That evening, after shaking off the ordeal of the television reporters, Noah and I had a delectable dinner of chicken cacciatore over brown rice pasta and broccoli spears. After barely finishing our last mouthfuls, we ran up to his bedroom, where I suited up and we paid homage to the amorous missionaries. Noah clutched at my back and buttocks, welcoming me inside then begging for more until he possessed all of me, including my heart. As we made love in Noah's four-poster bed next to a raging fire, we kissed again and again, leading to a colossal climax.

Afterward, Noah rested his head on my chest and we cuddled under Noah's thick white quilt comforter.

I kissed the top of his beautiful mane of hair, and asked, "What are your parents like?"

After kissing both of my pectoral muscles and licking my nipples, he responded, "They're typical people from Wisconsin. Homey, warm, sweet. My dad is a dairy farmer, and my mom is a bookkeeper. You'd like them."

"I do already. They made *you*."

Noah played with the dark hair on my chest.

"Are they supportive about your sexual orientation?" I asked.

"Totally. When I was thirteen I told them I was gay. They said, 'God doesn't make mistakes, so if he made you gay then you're supposed to be gay.'"

I held him tighter in my arms. "Do you have any brothers or sisters?"

"Just me. How about you, Nicky?"

"One brother who my parents say got the looks in the family."

Noah pretended to get up. "See you around. I'm going to meet your *brother*."

After slapping his bottom then hugging him tighter, I said, "My folks own a bakery back in Kansas. My brother works for them. He has a wife who works there too, and a daughter who will work there when she's of age. They're simple, good, kind people."

"They're fine with you?" Noah asked with a raised eyebrow.

"I was fifteen when I told them. A later bloomer than you."
He pinched my abs.

I explained. "They said they will always love me no matter what I am or what I do, as long as I give them grandchildren."

Noah looked up and smiled. "We'll have to work on that."

"Indeed."

After a tender kissing session, Noah asked, "What kind of kid were you?"

"Quiet, studious, a bit of a loner. I was on the wrestling team in high school."

He giggled. "I'll bet you liked getting in and out of those positions with the other boys."

"I still do. Here let me show you a few."

After a few holds and a fantastic release with Noah, I said, "Things changed when I found the local community theater. Then all hell broke loose."

He nodded. "Like every other gay kid."

"Only the *thespians*," I added.

"What was your first role on stage?"

I blushed. "I played Tiny Tim in *A Christmas Carol*."

Obviously thinking back to our recent lovemaking session, Noah smirked. "You sure aren't *Tiny* Tim now."

I pinched his nose, "What was your first role in a show?"

Noah responded proudly, "Captain Hook in *Peter Pan*."

"Hook." I patted his family jewels. "That fits."

We shared a knowing laugh.

I continued. "It always confused me why Peter Pan was played by a woman."

After another joint laugh, I looked at my gorgeous new lover, and said, "You must have been a cute little kid."

"The cutest." Noah unleashed his baby blue eyes, rosy red lips, pearly white teeth, and golden curly locks. "I had a stuffed elephant that never left my side."

"Hmm, an elephant has a long trunk. Have you talked to anyone about that?"

"And I was into gymnastics. My favorite was the pummel horse."

I replied a la a German psychiatrist, "I think we need to explore both of these issues."

Noah winked seductively. "Me, too."

That led to us exploring every inch of one another's bodies with massaging, kissing, and nibbling. Our exploration ended with Noah using his tongue to lead me to an oral orgasm the heights of which I had never experienced before. I returned the favor, and we fell asleep in one another's welcoming arms.

* * *

The next morning after a two-way vanilla mango scrub in the shower, and Greek yogurt with fruit (and nuts and vitamins for me) for breakfast, we finished our morning classes at the college then drove in my car to David's funeral.

The enormous gothic church was full of thick marble columns adorned with elaborate gold molding next to posted signs soliciting donations for the poor. David's large white coffin was positioned on the vast marble altar (rivaling Liberace's). Bouquets of multicolored flowers filled the church, as did David's family, colleagues, and friends. As this was not an open and affirming Christian church, Noah and I sat toward the rear, waiting to see if the fires of Hell (or a church worker) would devour us. No such luck. Noah and I nearly dozed off as the priest led a terminally long mass with altar boys being instructed to wave incense (hopefully that was all they were instructed to wave) accompanied by a choir droning hymn after hymn. Ariella sat in the front pew on the left side of the church with a young man who I assumed was her son, and Loptu Lee sat in the front pew on the right side of the church. This appeared to anger Ariella, as well as a number of other women dispersed throughout the church pews who Noah and I surmised were David's past or present lovers.

Tyler had actually shaved and pulled his hair back in a ponytail for the event. He displayed an angel tattoo on his arm as he led the students in Treemeadow's Christian Fellowship Club in a prayer about living the way God wants us to live. Thinking of David, Noah and I couldn't help but chuckle under our breaths.

The students playing the lead roles in my play, Paul, Ricky, Jan, and Kayla, occasionally leaned over to speak to Kyle until Ariella shushed them.

At the (finally!) completion of the ceremony, Martin rose to give the eulogy. Barely able to be seen behind the pulpit, our department head adjusted his black bowtie and sweater vest, cleared his throat, and said, "David Samson was a very good Scenic Designer. He was my colleague. David felt passionately about many things. He also shared many of his thoughts with the other professors in our department. He was advisor to our students' Christian Fellowship Club. He was also a husband, father, and intimate friend who was loved by *many*."

By this time, Noah and I were laughing so hard we felt like kids in Catechism class. When Martin finished his speech, Ariella then Kyle were called to the pulpit. Each spoke briefly and vaguely about David as a husband and father. When they were finished, the priest asked if anyone else would like to share his or her feelings about David. To everyone's surprise, Loptu rose and stood behind the pulpit. Wearing her usual black and white clothing with her black and white triangular hair, our split personality Playwriting professor fit in well with the ambiance of the church, until she spoke.

"David Samson was a warm, loving, and caring man."

Loptu's eyebrows rose upward, and she continued with a snarl on her heavily made up face. "But David changed on a dime." She pointed to the casket. "After this man met Millie Rodriguez, he turned into Satan himself!" She raised her arms into the crucifix position. "David stole something from me...my *heart*!"

The audience gasped. The priest stopped gazing at the altar boys and rushed to the pulpit in an attempt to stifle Loptu.

Loptu popped a green pill in her mouth and continued angelically. "I will always remember David as a wonderful man who I will miss dearly."

As Loptu walked back to her seat, there was a collective sigh from the audience.

The guests piled out of the church. As Noah and I offered our condolences to Ariella on the reception line, I noticed that Kyle, instead of standing next to his mother, was near a confessional chatting with Paul, Ricky, Jan, and Kayla from my show.

Later that afternoon, after our classes, Noah and I met in the Voice and Diction classroom. Since Millie Rodriguez's parents had flown her body back to Cuba, and Millie had no family in the area, Martin planned a farewell tribute for Millie in her classroom at the college.

Scotty led the Forensics Team students in reciting a poem in Millie's honor after which my graduate assistant flirted with the cater waiters. Martin rose to stand behind the podium in front of Millie's colleagues and students to give the eulogy (his second for the day). Our department head mentioned Millie's dedication to her field, adoration from her students, and loving heart (obviously for David).

When Martin concluded, Noah and I were the first inhabitants of the snack table. As I reached for a cheese Danish, Shayla slapped my hand, and whispered to me, "Don't let yourself go just because you finally hooked a man, Nicky." She handed me an apple instead.

Noah, true to form, chose a banana.

As I cased the room, I noticed that Ariella was not in attendance. I also spotted Jackson Grier arguing with Loptu by the window. When Loptu stormed out of the classroom, Noah asked me to follow him (Yes, anywhere!), and we landed down the hall in Loptu Lee's office.

Our Playwriting colleague sat on a small cherry red sofa sipping jasmine tea. Noah and I sat on a red leather bench next to the cherry wood fireplace. With her full black and white triangular-shaped hair, black slacks, and white blouse,

Loptu looked like a giraffe resting in a rose bush.

"Thank you for bringing me the curriculum modification reports, Noah, but you could have just emailed them."

"We wanted to talk to you," I said.

"So you two are an item now?" Loptu asked.

Looking like bookends, Noah and I faced one another then asked in unison, "How did you know?"

Loptu rested her tea cup on a tiny end table next to the sofa. "I'm a writer. I can sense things about people. You two have that, we just had sex look. It's in your eyes." Her eyes scanned downward. "And in your pants."

After moving in front of my ample package, Noah said, "Loptu, as you know I'm Detective Manuello's top suspect for the three murders on campus."

She laughed. "You didn't do it, Noah."

Squeezing Noah's hand, I responded, "He certainly didn't."

Loptu's eyebrows rose and her eyes bulged out of her head. "Isn't that what I just said? Are you calling me a liar, Nicky? Just because you two finally got it on, do you think you can come in here and threaten me with your two against one sick routine!"

Opening the tiny triangular shaped purse on her end table, Loptu clutched at a blue pill and popped it into her mouth. Once the jasmine tea had washed it down her throat, Loptu smiled at us warmly. "So, chums, what did you want to talk to me about?" Before we responded, Loptu looked at the papers on her desk and laughed. "I had my students write ten-minute plays about the murders. Nearly every one of them wrote *me* as the murderer."

Sitting at the edge of her sofa, I asked, "Did you know that David was stealing grant money from the college?"

"Sure. Didn't everyone?"

Noah added, "And that he was blackmailing Jackson?"

"That I didn't know. Why?"

I snuck a silencing look at Noah.

Noah responded, "Sorry, but we can't tell you, Loptu."

Loptu's face hardened. "So I'm supposed to tell you everything that *I* know, but you won't share what you know with *me*? You don't trust me? You think I'm a stupid woman incapable of keeping a secret! You both hate women! You hate heterosexuals! You hate Asians! You are both disgusting bigots!"

After popping two more pills in her mouth, Nice-Loptu was back with a warm glow in our direction.

Noah-as-Watson asked, "What were you and Jackson arguing about at Millie's tribute earlier today?"

Loptu responded cordially, "Jackson was badmouthing David. I was defending him. It's not right to talk against the dead, except for Millie."

Noah asked, "What was it like dating David?"

After smiling nostalgically, Loptu responded, "David was amazing in bed. He was completely hairless—head, chest, back, legs. I loved holding onto his smooth, muscular butt when he made love to me." She looked at David's picture on her fireplace mantel. "He was also a total chauvinist, which I also loved. He took care of me, protected me, but he treated me like dirt. I loved that too. I would have killed for David."

Trying to erase the thought from my memory of David and Loptu making love, I asked, "Was Ariella jealous when David left her for you?"

She laughed wickedly. "David told me Ariella was devastated. Of course he loved it. So did I."

I responded, "David liked having two women fighting over him?"

"Having two women *in love* with him. David felt it was his prerogative as a man, as the hunter, as the Y chromosome," Loptu explained.

Noah slid to the edge of the bench. "Did Ariella ever get over David?"

"I don't think so. But I can't blame her. Neither have I."

Holmes was on the case. "Why did you and David break up?"

She laughed. "*We* didn't break up. David broke up with

me."

"Why?"

Loptu's face turned sour. "Our Voice and Diction professor sweet talked him."

Noah asked, "Why couldn't David have all three of you?"

I hope you aren't a Mormon, Noah!

Loptu responded, "I would have taken a third of David rather than none of him. But Millie was the jealous type. So David went with his most *youthful* option. Unfortunately it wasn't me."

Trying to be as delicate as possible, I asked, "Do you know why David and Millie were not on good terms before David's death?"

Loptu's back hunched and Naughty-Loptu resurfaced. "What do you think I am a moron? Are you saying I wasn't compassionate about Millie's plight? Are you calling me insensitive? You think I'm a monster!"

Two more pills and Nice-Loptu was reborn. "I felt badly for Millie. It's never easy to terminate a pregnancy, even when the father wants no part of it."

Noah rose and rested his knee on the bench. "Were David and his son Kyle involved in some kind of activity together?"

She nodded, and her hair didn't budge. "They were involved in something that made David a great deal of money."

"What was it?" I asked.

With a twitch of a shoulder, Nasty-Loptu made her reentrance. "What do you want me to do? Kidnap Kyle and use water boarding techniques to force him to tell me what he and his father were up to? Do you think I am sadistic? Do you think I have a mean side like David!"

Loptu popped a red wonder into her mouth. Suddenly, she gasped, and fell face down on the floor. Noah leapt to her side and quickly checked the pulse in her neck. With a horrified look on his handsome face, Noah shouted, "Both Loptus are dead!"

CHAPTER SEVEN

The next morning the theatre faculty — those of us still alive — were back at the department's conference table staring at the empty seats around us, wondering who would be next. Despite the obvious mood of gloom and doom, I couldn't help thinking fondly about my second night with Noah.

We had barely finished dinner when Noah brought our dessert fixings up to his bedroom, where he and I created a terrific banana split — in more ways than one. Noah may be allergic to nuts in his food, but he certainly likes licking, nibbling, and devouring them in his bed.

After cuddling all night in Noah's antique four-poster, I woke to the smell of hot oatmeal with almonds (only for me) and raisins and cinnamon on a bed tray, and Noah's warm and loving good morning kiss. After breakfast, a shower, and a quick but passionate lovemaking session on the four-poster, we dressed and headed off to Treemeadow.

Sitting at his usual spot at the head of the table, Martin appeared to have aged five years since our last meeting. It was clear that the murders were taking a huge toll on him.

My faculty colleagues shifted in their seats, looking at the cathedral ceiling or the stained-glass window in an effort to avoid eye contact with one another. Even Shayla appeared concerned as she drew a noose on her minutes pad.

Finally, looking like a frazzled Buddha, Detective Manuello stood in front of the large window separating us from the growing mound of reporters, whose latest stories *alleged* that Noah and I were the new Leopold and Loeb. Manuello rubbed his sizeable stomach then began the meeting. "Thank you all for coming."

We came all right. I squeezed Noah's knee under the table and he blushed.

Manuello continued. "Given the tragic series of events in this department, we have no alternative but to close down the two Theatre Department buildings on campus."

Ariella flicked back her long black hair and we could almost see her eyes. "How can we teach our classes if the buildings are closed, detective?"

The look on Manuello's face said he would open up Fort Knox for Ariella Samson...if she'd open up for him.

Leaning on the mantel of the large stone fireplace, Detective Dickerson scratched at the ginger stubble on his baby face. "We explained to Professor Anderson that for the safety of your students, and for your own safety, all classes will need to be cancelled until further notice."

"I am terribly sorry, Mrs. Samson," Manuello said to Ariella personally.

"What about the play?" Tyler looked like a diabetic child in a candy factory.

Dickerson pleaded with Manuello. "Can't they still do the play? I'll bet it's terrific! Nicky is such a good director." Dickerson winked at me. My heart did a giddy somersault when Noah growled at him like a pit bull.

Rubbing his forehead in exasperation, Manuello replied, "The play will go on when I am assured that no one will get hurt. Until then all activities are on hold."

Scotty asked Manuello, "Can we still have committee meetings? After all, we're meeting right now." He put his hand on Noah's shoulder, and *I* growled.

Holding the cross around his neck, Tyler added, "The same goes for student club meetings. It's the right thing to do!"

A varicose vein away from breaking a blood vessel, Manuello shouted, *"Everything,* and that means *everything* that goes on in the two theatre buildings on this campus is cancelled until further notice."

Martin rose on shaky legs, and said sadly, "Nobody is sorrier about this than me, people. But given the loss of our colleagues, this seems like the only thing to do."

Resting his elbows on the table and planting his chin on his hands, Jackson asked, "How many more members of this department have to die before you figure out who is killing us off like plastic ducks at an arcade, detective?"

Gazing at Jackson with lust in his eyes, Scotty said, "I agree with Jackson."

Shayla wrote to Martin on her minutes pad, 'Somebody needs to put that kid in a cold shower...alone.'

My inner Sherlock Holmes kicked in. "We need to think about what our four colleagues had in common, and what got them killed."

"Right."

"We need answers now."

"On television they'd have had this solved in an hour."

As the murmur of the faculty built to a crescendo, Martin waved his small hands, and said, "Colleagues, friends, please, go to your offices, take what you need, and go home until I tell you it is safe to return to your classes. Each of you will be paid, and no sick days will be charged."

"I will be doing another press conference later today." Detective Manuello added with a glare in Noah's direction, "That means you *shouldn't!*"

My colleagues slowly left the conference room and grumbled to their offices.

At the doorway, Detective Dickerson put his hand on my shoulder. "Sorry about your play, Nicky. If there is *anything* that I can do —"

Noah took my hand, and said, "I know something you can do, detective. You and your superior can arrest the murderer."

Smirking like a teenager on medical marijuana, Dickerson responded, "We've narrowed down our list of suspects, and wouldn't you know, you're still on it, Professor Oliver. I guess that's because you seem to be at each of the four crime scenes!"

"You're barking up the wrong professor, Dickerson," I said before leading Noah out the door.

"I don't like the way he looks at you. And it kills me that Manuello and Dickerson still think *I'm* the murderer."

I put my arm around him. "Please refrain from using the word, *kills*, will you, lover?"

With nobody left in the hallway but us, Noah melted in my arms, and asked tentatively, "Is that what we are, Nicky? Lovers?"

I responded, "As our students would say, 'um like totally.'"

We kissed then kissed again then again.

Coming up for air, Noah asked, "As much as I'd love to spend my days…and nights with you in bed, what about our investigation?"

I thought a moment. "I think we need to talk to Martin."

"Lead the way, Sherlock."

Noah and I ran into Shayla in the hallway outside of Martin's office. Having already put on her fur-lined red coat and black boots, she looked like Mrs. Klaus — if the Klaus' was an interracial marriage.

"Now don't you two go and get married during our time off and not invite me," she said.

"It's a deal," said Noah with a kiss on my cheek.

Shayla chuckled. "I hate weddings, but I'll go to yours. There's something about two men getting married that I like."

I asked, "What's that?"

"It's totally *hot*." She laughed loudly and left the building.

As we approached Martin's office, we heard voices coming from inside. Noah motioned for us to leave and come back later. I waved Noah forward and we took Shayla's usual spot at the doorway, peeking into Martin's office.

Martin sat at his desk and Scotty Bruno stood in front of him like a filet mignon in a butcher's window. Wearing his usual four-season tank top and shorts, Scotty pretended to drop a piece of paper from Martin's desk, so he could bend over in Martin's direction. As he rose to put the paper back on the desk, Scotty flexed each of his bulging arm and chest muscles in Martin's direction. Then Scotty stood above Martin and moved his sock enhanced crotch near Martin's face. Noah and I looked at one another in disbelief.

"Thank you for agreeing to speak with me, Martin."

"Everyone in the department knows my door is always open."

Scotty spoke like Lolita after a sex change operation. "That's what I wanted to talk to you about."

My graduate assistant and my department head sat on two of the tall, leather wingback chairs flanking the fireplace as Noah and I listened attentively in the doorway.

"I really enjoy teaching Millie's classes. And I think I'm a good teacher."

"I agree," said Martin.

Putting his hand on Martin's knee, Scotty said, "And I love serving on Millie's faculty committee, and advising the Forensics Club."

"Good."

Scotty leaned over and flexed his pectoral muscles inches away from Martin's nose. "So, I am wondering if when everything is…settled and back to normal, can I come on board…permanently?"

That little vixen!

Martin smiled. "When it comes time to replace our departed colleagues, we will have a public search. You can certainly apply for whichever position you feel fits you the most."

Scotty rose from his seat, sat on Martin's lap, and put his arms around him. "But why do a search when I'm already *here*, and so successful, and so completely willing to do *whatever* is asked of me?"

"College protocol calls for a search."

"Then how about you search me right now?" Scotty rested Martin's hands on his biceps then kissed Martin square on the mouth.

Martin abruptly stood up and Scotty fell back landing on the floor, just inches from the fire. "Scotty, what do you think you're doing?"

Scrambling to his feet, Scotty picked up the sock that had dislodged from his shorts. "I was just trying to —"

"I know what you were *just trying to do* and you should be ashamed of yourself, young man!" Martin said angrily. "Is that all you think of yourself? Is that all you think of *me*? I'm three times your age with a husband and two grown daughters. If you don't respect yourself or me or this college, at least respect *their* feelings."

Scotty got to his feet, pushing back tears. "I'm sorry, Martin. It's just so hard nowadays to get a tenure track position."

"Well this is definitely not the way to get one in *my* department!"

With tears skiing off his turned-up nose, Scotty said, "I know I messed up, Martin. You must hate me now. I wanted a job so badly that I screwed up my only hope of ever getting a full-time position in academia!"

Martin's face softened. "Sit down."

They faced one another on the leather chairs.

After a sigh, Martin said, "I remember being your age and so desperately wanting so many things, and wanting them immediately. Scotty, what I learned was that achieving your goals…being successful only matters if you really work for it…and if you deserve it."

Scotty wiped his eyes on Martin's lavender cloth napkin. "I've worked so hard. And the students really learn from me."

"Then trust that your abilities will be what bring you success. Getting there any other way takes the fun out of it. Believe me, I know."

Scotty did a double-take. "You?"

After a chuckle, Martin said, "Believe it or not, Scotty, I was once young and cute. Even cuter than you."

They shared a smile.

Martin turned back the pages of time. "When I was a temporary full-time instructor at another college, an *opportunity*...presented itself to become department head, provided that I was willing to...be a good *sport* with the college president."

Scotty sat at the edge of his chair like a kid at the circus. "What did you do?"

"I thought about it, and then I asked myself, how happy would I be with my success knowing how I got that job. What would my colleagues think of me? What would my family think of me? What would *I* think of me?"

Scotty nodded in understanding. "And years later you became department head on your own merit here at Treemeadow."

Martin winked at him. "You got it, kid."

Putting his head in his hands, Scotty moaned. "I feel like such a fool."

Martin put his arm around Scotty and walked him to the door like Andy Hardy and the Judge. Noah and I hid behind Shayla's desk.

"Scotty, we all behave like fools now and again. The secret is to not have too many agains."

They paused at the door.

"I apologize, Martin. I promise this will never happen again."

Martin replied, "It better not, young man."

"Thank you."

"Thank *you*, Scotty." Martin licked his lips, laughed, and went back into his office.

After Scotty was gone, Martin shouted, "You two can come in now."

Noah and I entered Martin's office, asking in unison, "How did you—?"

"I may be old, but I still have my peripheral vision. It comes in handy reading Shayla's notes at department meetings." Martin invited us to join him for hot cocoa at the fireplace.

Once seated with lavender cloth napkins on our laps and china cups in our hands, Martin said hopefully, "Have you two finally become an item?"

After some stammering, stuttering, and giggling, Noah and I answered in unison, "Yes."

"Thank goodness," said Martin looking like a proud father of the grooms as he gave each of us a warm hug.

"What gave us away?" Noah asked with a hand on my knee.

Martin looked at us as if seeing us for the time. "You both look...comfortable in your own skins. As if by finding each other, you've found yourselves. I'm so happy for you both." He raised his china cup to us.

Again we said in unison, "Thank you."

"Oh dear, now you two are even talking alike."

We all laughed.

After taking a warm sip of cocoa, I said, "My graduate assistant is obviously determined to get a job."

Noah added, "One way or another."

Martin stared at the dancing flames. "I don't envy young people today in the college job market." Martin took a sip of cocoa and wiped his mouth with a monogrammed napkin. "With colleges relying so heavily on adjunct instructors and graduate assistants, the tenure track jobs just aren't there any longer, at least not at the four-year universities."

With a pained look on his handsome face, Noah responded, "That's why I'm so concerned about my tenure hearing."

I put my hand on Noah's shoulder. "Noah, the only tenured faculty members left in the department are Martin, Ariella, Jackson, and me. Martin is running unopposed for department head now. You'll have no problem getting tenure with David and his girlfriends out of the picture." I covered my mouth then said to Martin, "I didn't mean it that way."

"I know, Nicky." The orange glow of the fire illuminated the worry in Martin's face. "I never thought I would lose *four* of my children. I've done three eulogies in one week."

I hit my head. "Martin, Noah and I forgot about Wally's funeral."

Martin's face clouded with grief. "The funeral was an understandably small affair. Wally's niece emailed vague instructions from Texas about burying him anywhere we like, accompanied by detailed instructions on how his belongings should be sent to her. We had a little ceremony for Wally in the college chapel and buried him in the cemetery with the words, 'When I was department head...' on his tombstone." Martin smiled. "That was Shayla's touch."

"Who came from the college?" Noah and I asked in unison.

Martin's eyes rolled back in his small head like a toy slot machine. "Some emeritus faculty...and Jackson was there. He told me he wanted to make sure, 'the old coot was really dead.'"

After another sip of cocoa, I said, "We found out why David was blackmailing Jackson."

Noah added, "What business was it of David's that Jackson had sexual reassignment surgery to correct his gender?"

Martin responded, "Obviously it was *big* business for David."

Noah asked, "Did you know that David stole grant money from the college, and that Wally stole office supplies from the department?"

Letting out an elongated sigh, Martin responded, "Of course. When I confronted them, they denied it. I had only hearsay. No tangible proof."

Watson switched course with, "When is Loptu's funeral?"

"Loptu's brother said her will calls for immediate cremation with no memorial of any kind," Martin answered.

"I'd have thought she'd have *two* funerals," I said with a gleam in my eye. This led to Noah's stifled guffaw in my direction.

Fighting the giggles, I asked, "Is there word yet on the cause of Loptu's death?"

Martin filled in the missing piece on the last murder.

"Detective Manuello informed me after the meeting today that Loptu was poisoned in the same manner as Wally."

Rubbing his forehead, Noah said, "Since our offices are all in the Theatre Arts Building, each of us had access to Loptu during the five to twelve hours before the rat poison took effect."

Back in Sherlock mode, I asked, "How did Ariella react to Loptu's wacky speech at David's funeral?"

Martin shrugged his small shoulders, adjusted his lavender sweater vest then wiped his mouth with his lavender cloth napkin. "You know me — I'm the last person to gossip."

And I'm the last person at the dessert bar. "At David's funeral, did you speak with David's son, Kyle?"

Martin strained his memory. "As I recall, Kyle spent most of the time speaking with some of the students from your play, Nicky."

Looking at the department budget sheets on Martin's desk, I asked, "Do you know if David, Wally, Millie, and Loptu had wills?"

Martin nodded. "As a matter of fact, Detective Dickerson showed them to me. When Dickerson asked for our department's budget, salaries, and other expenditures for his investigation, I said to the detective, 'You show me *yours*, and I'll show you *mine*.'"

That sounds familiar.

Watson asked, "Who gets David's money in his will?"

"Ariella… and David's son," Martin answered.

Leaving no will unopened, I asked, "How about Wally, Millie, and Loptu?"

Martin struggled with how many beans he should let out of the pot, and happily turned the pot upside down. "Wally left his money to his grandnephew. Millie and Loptu both left their assets to David."

I smirked. "Ariella told me David grew up poor, and he spent a great deal of his adult life trying to make up for that by gathering huge sums of money. I guess this is how he did it."

Noah sat on the edge of his seat, "Martin, who gets Millie's and Loptu's assets upon David's death?"

As if having not thought about it before, Martin responded, "I assume David's heirs."

I nearly fell off my chair. "Ariella told me she wanted no part of David's relentless quest for wealth."

Noah rested his head back on his chair. "Whether she wants it or not, Nicky, it looks like she's *got* it."

I corrected him (not a good habit). "She and *Kyle*, that is."

CHAPTER EIGHT

With our unexpected sabbaticals from teaching, the next morning Noah and I closed the bedroom curtains to the reporters outside and rested in bed playing footsies and feeding one another French toast smothered with strawberries (and pistachio nuts for me).

"Did I ever tell you I like the cleft in your chin?" Noah asked with lust in his blue eyes.

"Is that the only thing you like about me?"

"No. I also like your long, thick...sideburns."

I responded with narrow eyes. "Are my sideburns the only long, thick thing about me that you like?"

His eyes danced. "I really like your...fingers, and your...feet." He squeezed my manhood. "Oh, and I like *this* too."

"And here I thought you liked me for my great wit, incredible mind, kind heart, and because I'm crazy about you."

He finally said it. "I *love* you for those things."

"I *love* you too." *It feels so liberating, and so wonderful.*

We locked eyes and hands.

"So what are we going to do about this?"

"Gee, I don't know," I said tongue-in-cheek—leading to my tongue all over Noah's body and his all over mine.

A half hour later we showered the strawberry juice off our bodies, and regrouped in my large, Victorian style kitchen. Dressed in my sweat clothes and vowing to go to the gym (later), I loaded dishes into the dishwasher (obviously a much welcome addition the Victorians didn't have). Noah sat at the breakfast nook grading papers.

"Noah, this feels really good."

Adding a final minus five on Kayla's paper (no doubt from her staring at Paul during the test), Noah said, "I know! I feel guilty saying it, but I can really use this break."

Swallowing a handful of vitamins with a cranberry juice chaser, I responded, "I don't mean Detective Manuello closing down our department. Though I agree this break is much needed for grading, assessment, and course planning." *Sorry for the academic plug.* "I mean you and me cooking, working, showering, sleeping, and *not* sleeping together. It feels so *right.*"

Noah dropped his paper and was at my side in a flash. "I can't believe how easy and wonderful it has been."

"You were expecting that I'd be a grouch and a slob?" I pinched his behind.

Cuddling up to me and wrapping his arms around my back, Noah said adoringly, "I dreamed about this... fantasized about this for so long. I can't believe it's all real."

"How's this to help convince you?"

After enjoying a lovemaking session next to the double sink, we thanked the Victorians for making sturdy countertops. Then feeling the after-effects of our passion, I massaged my groin muscles, and Noah applied aloe vera juice to his red backside.

"Noah, will you move in with me?"

Before I got out the last word, Noah was in my arms and I was running my hands over his silky blond curls, V-shaped back, and firm (but sore) buttocks.

"I thought you'd never ask me."

"I thought you would be hesitant."

"Why?"

"Noah, the college provides a furnished house for *each* faculty member."

"So we can use the second house for parties."

"Meaning *your* house."

He batted his eyes at me. "Why can't we move into *my*

house?"

"My house is bigger than yours."

He brushed his thigh against my still aching groin. "Not only is your *house* bigger."

I slipped my hands down the back of his jeans and squeezed...gently. "How about you move your things in here today, and we see how it goes?"

"Deal." He kissed my nose.

"Noah, maybe we should tell our families and friends first."

He giggled. "I already posted on Facebook as 'in a relationship.'"

I had to admit it. "Me too."

After sharing a laugh, he said, "My family can't wait to meet you."

"Same here."

Noah had a wild gleam in his eyes. "Let's schedule a trip to Kansas and a trip to Wisconsin. And let's plan a big party here and invite all of our friends."

I held him closer. "Slow down. Four of our colleagues have been murdered. This is a college town. We need to find the murderer." I added with a twinkle in my eyes. "And restore safety and justice to Gotham City."

A guilty look overtook Noah's sweet face. "You're right, Nicky. How could I be so selfish?"

Lifting his chin, I answered, "You're not being selfish. We deserve to be happy. *Everybody* deserves to be happy. But right now, we need to protect our colleagues...and ourselves from this sicko."

As committed as a shut-in sending her social security check to a tax-exempt religious television network, Noah said, "Count me in."

The ring of my cell phone startled us. After the murders in our department, lots of things startled us. Noah went back to grading his papers at the kitchen nook, and I took the call in the upstairs study.

Upon entering the study, I walked up the two steps and

sat on the window seat. Staring out the picture window, I looked at the house's white picket fence and trellis leading to a furry white lawn surrounded by gorgeous silver evergreen trees. The voice on the other end of the line brought me back to reality and to Treemeadow College.

"Nicky, it's Ariella."

"Hi, Ariella. Enjoying your time off?"

After some shuffling noises, Ariella was back. "Sorry...I was pressing Jan's new dress for Act I."

I sat back on a pillow and rested my feet on the other end of the window seat. "You're in the Costume Shop?"

"Of course." She responded as if a five-year-old asked her if fish swim.

"Detective Manuello banned us from going inside the two theatre buildings on campus."

She sighed. "I shouldn't have to remind you that the show will go up eventually."

"The show is in great shape, including the costumes."

As if talking to one of her students, Ariella said, "Costumes are living, breathing things. They need to be aired out, washed, pressed, and hung up correctly."

Feeling a chill from the window, I moved to the green tiled fireplace. After lighting a fire, I sat in the tall green recliner flanking it. "Are Detective Manuello and his stooge there?"

After a pause, she responded, "It's pretty quiet. I think I'm the only one here."

Tentacles of fear crept up my back. "Listen to me. Hang up Jan's costume, and get out of there."

"Why?"

"Because four of our colleagues have been murdered! You could be next."

"I locked myself inside the Costume Shop. Nothing can harm me in here, except maybe the chemicals in the fabric dyes."

"Are the windows shut and locked?"

After a pause, she replied, "Like Fort Knox."

I breathed again. "All right, but promise me that if you

hear or see *anyone*, you'll call Manuello immediately."

Ariella said, "I didn't call to worry you."

Too late.

"I'm not happy with Paul's cape for the show. It doesn't flow easily on stage. I want to make a new one using lighter fabric."

"Do we have time for that?" I asked while stoking the fire.

"Nicky, we have nothing *but* time."

"Have you told Paul?"

"Actually, yes. I was visiting Kyle in the Film Department, and Paul was there with Ricky, Jan, and Kayla."

That caught my attention. "What were our theatre students doing in the Film Department?"

"With our department closed, they were probably looking for somewhere to go." She let out a long stream of air, or maybe it was the costume steamer. "So can I build a new cape?"

"Of course. Do you have the fabric?"

She sounded as if pins were in her mouth. "I bought the material earlier today. I think it will work perfectly."

Not so fast, Professor. "Ah, I want to tell you again how sorry I am about David."

"No you're not." She laughed and hopefully didn't swallow a pin. "It's okay, Nicky. I know you didn't like David. I didn't like him much myself these last few years. He was struggling with a lot of demons. I hope he's at peace."

I rested back on the recliner. "I know this is none of my business—"

"That's never stopped anyone before in our department."

I laughed. "Martin told me that David left everything to you...and to Kyle. I just want to say that I'm glad."

"Why? You want us to take you out to dinner?"

Forget costuming, Ariella. You should be a stand-up comic. "I disagreed with a lot of things David did when he was alive, but honoring his wife and son in his will was not one of them."

She seemed legitimately touched. "Thanks, Nicky. I

appreciate that."

"Martin also told me that Loptu and Millie mentioned David in their wills."

She cleared her throat in agitation. "So I heard."

I sat behind my oak roll top desk and took notes on what she was saying. "Ariella, with David deceased, do you and Kyle inherit *their* money as well?"

"That's what their lawyers told me."

"You spoke to their lawyers?"

"They contacted me earlier today."

"Does Kyle know?"

"I told him, but Kyle doesn't care about anything except his latest student film."

On a roll, I asked, "I wonder if Loptu's brother and Millie's parents will contest their wills?"

"I would if I were them."

"With our weakening faculty contract, the extra money will no doubt come in handy for you."

"Is there anyone who thinks he has enough money, Nicky?"

Good point. "David's funeral was amazing." *It was amazing all right.*

"Thanks." Was she wiping her eyes?

"Did you go to Wally's funeral?"

"Are you kidding?"

"What do you mean?" *Do tell, girl!*

She sounded like a junkie describing her rehab counselor. "When Wally was department head…"

I thought those words were killed along with Wally.

"…Wally didn't support David when David went up for tenure."

Like David didn't support my tenure…or Noah's.

Ariella continued bitterly. "With a young child at home, that made Wally number one villain in our house. It's hard to forget things like that, Nicky."

"How did David get tenure without his department head's support?" *And, I assume, without his colleagues' support?*

Obviously reliving a painful memory, Ariella responded, "David did some…research then blackmailed the members of the All College Promotion and Tenure Committee." She let out a sad laugh. "Everybody has secrets, Nicky."

Just like David blackmailed Jackson. "Back then Wally's name must have been mud to you…and to Kyle."

"*Mud* is being kind," she responded resentfully.

"I saw Kyle at David's funeral, but I've never met him at any of our plays. Does he come to the theatre buildings much?"

"Never," she responded with a sigh. "He's in his own celluloid world in the film building."

I probed like a urologist examining an enlarged prostate. "Was Kyle on good terms with Loptu and Millie?"

After a staccato guffaw, Ariella answered, "You directed *Death of a Salesman.* What kid likes his father's mistresses?"

I walked over to the fireplace and warmed my feet at the fire. "Didn't David ever take Kyle with him to visit Loptu or Millie?"

Amidst the noise of moving fabric, Ariella answered, "After having dinner out with David and Loptu, Kyle told me he wanted to 'kill the crazy bitch' and 'punch Dad out' for leaving me. When Kyle came home from dinner at Millie's, he said Millie was 'the most depressing charity case' he'd ever met. It didn't sound like it went too well."

I heard a loud bang. "Ariella, are you okay!"

"No worries. I dropped an iron, luckily not on my foot. I better go and get started on the new cape. I'll let you know when it's finished."

I no sooner hung up the phone when Noah came back with his car full of boxes. After we unpacked his things, Noah left for another round of the same as I worked on my syllabi and course materials for next semester.

As I was heading down the stairs to start dinner, I heard knocking at my front door. I opened it to find my frequently tardy student, P.J. Myers, shivering on my wraparound front porch.

"Hi um, Professor, I'm like sorry to bother you, but I was like wondering, you know, if I could talk to you and stuff like that?"

After I hung P.J.'s parka on the hall coat rack, we sat in my kitchen nook as P.J. focused on his apple spice herbal tea, and I focused on P.J.

"I've already said everything that I am going to say to you about your grade in Directing I. Perhaps you can use this time off to catch up on the assignments."

He nervously pulled at his nose ring. In a domino effect it tugged at the gold chain linking to his earring, which tugged at his earring, which tugged at his ear. "I like didn't come here to um talk about my grade and stuff like that."

After letting out a sigh of relief, I asked, "Then why are you here?"

P.J. looked down at the linoleum floor. "This is kinda like hard to say."

I leaned forward. "Neither of us is getting any younger, especially me."

P.J. shifted his tongue ring to one side of his mouth. "Professor, you like know how I um like Jan, and how I have been like giving her gifts and stuff like that?"

I nodded. *If you're here for advice on how to win over a girl, you've definitely come to the wrong professor.*

P.J. tried to run his fingers through his hair but realized that with it gelled straight up in the air that was impossible. "I kinda followed Jan to, you know, the Film Department." He rubbed the sweaty palms of his hands over his faded jeans. "Jan, Kayla, Ricky, and um Paul were kinda sitting, you know, on a um bench together in the like lounge there. I um sat on the like next bench, and um overheard them talking to um Kyle Samson about like being in Kyle's, you know, film and stuff like that."

"Okay?" *If Noah wants children, we will adopt them at thirty years old.*

Squirming in his seat, with all of P.J.'s jewelry he looked like a nervous reindeer tied to a sleigh. "Kyle and um your four theatre students said they had like filmed it, you know, in like Kyle's dorm room."

"And?" Outside the kitchen window, the sun was setting in ribbons of red, orange, purple, and yellow. I hoped Noah would get back soon. P.J. was a poor substitution.

After taking in a breath that filled his facial piercings, P.J. finally blurted it out. "It's kinda a porn film."

That obviously got my attention. "Are you saying Kyle is making an adult film starring *my* theatre students!"

P.J. nodded. "From like what I could um hear, it was like Kyle's idea. I think um Kyle's dad, before he was like totally killed, was, you know, doing the like producing and like marketing and stuff like that."

I nearly fell out of the breakfast nook. "Are you saying this isn't their first film?"

P.J. seemed ready to cry. "They um said it was their, you know, third."

My eyes bulged out of my head. "Their *third* porn film."

He nodded in embarrassment.

"Why are they doing this?"

He wiped his sweaty hands on his worn sweater. "Jan and Kayla like mentioned something, you know, about the high cost of like tuition and stuff like that." He grimaced. "And um about getting to like do um scenes with Paul. Kyle like talked about wanting his own um production company. Ricky like talked about um Paul. And Paul um talked, you know, about himself."

We were nose ring to nose. "Is there any possibility that my students were rehearsing for an acting class scene, or talking about a student film that takes place in the world of adult films — but isn't *actually* an adult film?"

P.J. shook his head, sounding like a wind chime. "The next day I was, you know, kinda outside the um door to the like editing suite in the like film building when they were, you know, inside the um suite like watching a kinda scene. At um one point Ricky um left for a like minute to, you know, use the um bathroom. So I kinda pretended to be like walking by and I kinda took a like peek inside.

"What did you see?"

He wiped a wad of perspiration from his neck. "On the um screen was Paul like in a bed, like naked, you know, with um Kayla and…" Tears rimmed his eyes. "…my Jan like naked too and um sitting on him while they…" He couldn't go on.

I handed P.J. a napkin from the napkin holder.

After wiping his eyes, careful not to draw blood from the ring in his eyelid, P.J. continued. "When um Ricky went back inside the like editing suite, I, you know, ducked around the um corner, and when Ricky like opened the door to, you know, go like back inside, I um looked in again. This like time they were like showing a um scene with Ricky like naked with, you know, his mouth on Paul's, you know."

It all makes sense now: Jan, Kayla, Ricky, and Paul with their heads together at rehearsals and in class complaining about the high cost of tuition, fawning all over Paul, and plotting something. Rising on shaky legs, I put my arm around P.J. and slowly walked him to the door. "Thank you for telling me about this, P.J. But please don't tell anyone else for now. Okay?"

"Um okay." At the coat rack, P.J. put on his parka and gloves. "Professor, will um Jan like get expelled and stuff like that?"

"I don't know what is going to happen."

He looked at me pleadingly. "Please don't like let Jan, you know, get hurt and stuff like that."

I replied, "I have the feeling I'm too late on that one."

After I opened the door, P.J. nodded sadly and went out into the cold, dark night.

CHAPTER NINE

Later that evening after Noah and I unpacked the rest of his things and finished dinner, we cuddled on the sofa under a patchwork quilt in the back parlor. Like the flames dancing in the stone fireplace before us, Noah and I wrapped our bodies around each other and glowed.

After a log crackled, I gazed into Noah's contented face, and said, "This is where you belong — next to me."

He kissed me then responded blissfully, "Always."

I gladly returned the kiss. "I can see the headlines in the newspaper tomorrow, 'Leopold moves in with Loeb to plan future murders at Treemeadow College.'"

"I think I'm more a Loeb, Nicky."

I nibbled on his earlobe. "I agree."

"What did you do all day while I was packing my things?" Noah asked.

"After talking to Ariella on the phone, I had a male visitor who told me something x-rated."

"Really?" Noah's claws unfurled.

"Back tiger." I took a sip of my vanilla rooibus tea. "P.J., the Film major in my Directing I class, told me that Kyle, David's son, directed porn movies on campus and David distributed them! And that Kyle is still carrying on the family tradition with Paul, Jan, Kayla, and Ricky as his porn stars!"

"Haven't they heard of working as student aides?" Noah asked incredulously.

"My guess is they make a lot more money as porn stars. Besides, P.J. didn't think money was their only motivation. He believes Ricky, Jan, and Kayla are doing it because they are hot for Paul, and Paul is doing it because he's hot to see himself on film."

Noah pulled his feet into his buttocks. "Don't they know that Kyle will have that film for the rest of their lives to do whatever...whenever he wants with it? Not to mention that any horny kid or adult can download them onto his or her computer."

I cocked my head. "How do you know so much about porn films?"

He smirked. "I've read about them on the internet."

I returned the smirk. "I've *read* about them too." Then I rested his head on my chest, and said like an old geezer, "Ah, kids today!"

The crease between Noah's eyebrows deepened. "Nicky, do you think Kyle's porn company has something to do with the murders?"

We sat up facing one another.

I tented my fingers a la Sherlock Holmes. "David didn't know he wouldn't live to reap the benefits of the company, or the two wills for that matter, but the murderer *did*. Noah, think about it, with David gone, who benefits from the porn business?"

"Kyle."

"Right! And who benefits from the financial scores in the three wills?"

His eyes lit up. "Ariella...and *Kyle*." Watson wasn't totally convinced. "I understand why Ariella or Kyle would want to kill Loptu and Millie for their money, but why would either of them want to kill Wally?"

I nodded. "Because Wally was department head, as he never let any of us forget, when David went for tenure. According to Ariella, Wally's lack of support for David's tenure enraged the entire family."

Noah took a sip of his blueberry lemongrass tea. "But why wait so long to take their revenge on Wally?"

I replied, "Wally knew about David stealing grant money and blackmailing the All College Promotion and Tenure

Committee to get tenure. So maybe Wally also knew about the adult film business!"

We sipped each other's teas as Noah processed the new information.

"I don't think we should report Kyle's porn company to Martin or to Detective Manuello... at least not yet."

"How come?"

Noah rested his chin on his fists. "I think we should investigate this first, on our own, to see if your theory is right."

I got up and stoked the fire. "Since we have who knows how much time off, I'm having a production meeting and line-through here to keep the play front and center in the cast and crew's brains. We can fish around about this then."

"Good idea."

"We can serve snacks and drinks, all nonalcoholic of course."

Noah said deviously, "Better rethink the alcohol. It loosens the tongue...and other things, or so I've heard."

"We can test that theory later tonight."

We shared a giggle.

Noah suddenly looked like a cherub possessed by a demon. "Nicky, I know something else you have to do."

"Is this something legal?"

"Sort of." With the flames bursting (in the fireplace and in Noah's head), Noah joined me at the fireplace mantel. "You've never actually *met* Kyle, have you?"

"No."

He rubbed his hands together over the fire like one of the witches in *Macbeth*. "I think it's time you do just that."

Noah's eyes lit up like grenades. "You are a director. I am an actor. We are professors at a college with a Costume Shop, Scene Shop, prop closet, and makeup tables."

"I don't understand."

He shook my shoulders. "Nicky, there's a murderer loose on this campus. Obviously the detectives' traditional methods of investigating, questioning, and using forensics have failed. So it is time for us to use *our* methods instead."

"Meaning?"

"Meaning, you Nicky Abbondanza and I Noah Oliver, thespians, are going to save our theatre department, and our college, by using the best weapons we have…the tools of our theatrical trade." With a mad gleam in his eyes and a clenched fist over his heart, Noah added, "*We* are going to nab the killer and end this business of murder…by using the business of *show*."

* * *

Over the next couple of days, Noah and I spoke to a few students living on the same dormitory floor as Kyle. After offering the students a gift…of twenty dollars cash each, they confirmed P.J.'s story about Kyle's *movie* company. Twenty more bucks got us the company name, and another twenty bought their silence.

When we got home (Noah called my house his home!), we headed for my study to go online to research Kyle's production company, As Young as You F___ Productions. After checking out Kyle's growing inventory of films, we sampled some of the scenes, strictly for professional purposes (though we spent a bit more time on the gay scenes than on the bi and straight scenes).

With Noah prompting me at my desk, I set up a fictitious email name and address, and emailed Kyle, via his production company, to request an audition for his next film. Kyle's immediate response was cautious, no doubt fearing that I was a member of local law enforcement or the campus police. When my next email casually mentioned the number nine and a quarter, Kyle's fears seemed to evaporate into visions of sugar daddies swarming his web site.

To prepare for my audition, Noah and I created a new persona for me. As we devised, *Butch* (my new stage name) was raised on a farm in Kansas. After Butch's father passed away from swine flu, the widow of the local bank president, whose husband had also succumbed to the dreaded disease, took Butch under her...wing. So Butch left his life of milking cows, herding sheep, feeding pigs, grooming horses, and pitching hay to accompany the grieving widow to achieve her heart's desire of getting a college education at Treemeadow College. Once in Vermont, Butch led the good life in a high class new condo until his sugar momma flunked out of Treemeadow and went back to Kansas to marry the new bank president. Having accompanied the recently engaged widow to the Vermont airport, Butch was in the airport men's room, voiding himself of his airport taco lunch, when his foot made the acquaintance of an anti-gay fundamentalist Tea Party Republican senator in the next stall. Butch and the Senator shared an enjoyable release, leading to a mutually satisfying relationship with Butch landing his own mini mansion in Treemeadow. Sadly, their relationship ended when the senator's wife came home to find her husband screaming, "Yee hah!" while bent over their young son's horsey with Butch, chaps down, standing behind the senator waving his cowboy hat and thrusting his hips. Having taken a shining to Treemeadow, and with nowhere else to go, Butch thanked his lucky stars when, while walking in the park next to the college, Butch met a Treemeadow College dorm monitor. After engaging in an orgy with the dorm monitor and his three roommates in their dorm room, the monitor told Butch about Kyle's...side business and recommended that Butch contact Kyle A.S.A.P. to show Kyle his...wares.

Standing stoically in my master bathroom with Noah on his knees in front of me (It's not what you think), I winced as Noah, with a look of determination in his eyes, raised my electronic razor and shaved my legs, butt, stomach, chest, back, arms, and pubic area (garnering a new level of trust between us) until the orange floor tile looked like a black forest.

Finally, Noah and I hit the Costume Shop, prop closet, and makeup tables in the theatre building on campus, which of course were vacant, and we quickly gathered everything we needed. After I got into costume, or rather into my get-up, I looked at my reflection in the Costume Shop mirror and burst out laughing. There before me was a tall, muscular, dark-haired cowboy wearing skin-tight button down blue jeans (sans underwear), worn brown cowboy boots, an open yellow and brown flannel shirt (two sizes too small) with pectoral muscles bulging out of it, a black (fake) mustache, and a black cowboy hat. I remembered my Kansas accent, and *Butch Whopper* was born.

An hour later I was standing in Kyle Samson's dorm room facing Kyle, and a digital movie camera. With his long, dark hair, morose expression, and tall limbs, Kyle was certainly Ariella's son. He no doubt got his lust for money and power, however, from his father.

After we shared some polite, forced conversation about my past, rather Butch Whopper's past, Kyle moved behind the tripod, clicked on the camera, and gave me his first direction.

"Please look toward the camera and say your name and age, Butch."

That's the first time anyone's ever called me butch. I looked at the camera, and said in my strongest Kansas dialect, "Howdy. Mah name's Butch Whopper, and ahm jest a cowboy from Kansas." *Think I laid it on a bit too thick?*

Kyle continued routinely. "Are you gay, straight, or bi?"

"Ahm one hunid per cent hetero, but after a little moonshine from ma daddy's still, I often fahnd maself rollin' around in the hay with one of mah male cousins, if ya know what ah mean?" I winked at the camera. "So ah guess ahm bisexual, meanin', ya come bah me and ah'll get sexual." I tipped my cowboy hat at the camera hoping my fake mustache wouldn't fall off.

Kyle continued. "How old are you?"

"Ah will be twenty-fav yirs old tomorra." *If I find a way to time travel back ten years.*

Disappearing behind the camera, Kyle asked, "Why do you want to be in my movies?"

My heart pounded in my chest. "Your dorm monitor fellas and gals told me you was a great director. Basides, ah need the money lahk a horse needs brushin' after a storm."

Kyle seemed undaunted by my over the top performance. "Why do you need money, Butch?"

I felt like a rodeo rider on top of a neurotic horse. "See I got nobody in Vermont 'cept yours truly. And ahd lahk to register fur some of them classes at your college."

Appearing to buy my act, or perhaps hoping his patrons would buy it, Kyle panned out of my close-up shot and settled on a full figure shot. "Please slowly take off your hat then your shirt."

Somehow my sweaty hands threw off my hat then unbuttoned my shirt and tossed it onto Kyle's bed.

"Good. Now take off your boots."

I kicked them off as my lunch made its way up my esophagus.

"All right, now slowly take off your pants."

After my shaking hands unbuttoned the fly of my jeans, I dropped my pants. My hope was that Paul and Ricky, though younger and more muscular, didn't quite measure up to Butch Whopper in the dick department.

Kyle's jaw dropped to the sperm-stained rug below. "Good. Ah...now please jerk off toward the camera then cum when I say, 'Go.'"

As I looked in the direction of Kyle's voice, his camera moved...and Kyle's desk blurred into the window. Before I knew it, the room grew dark, and little white stars danced in front of me as I hit the floor. Butch Whopper's porn career had begun and ended with a dorm room screen test.

The next thing I remembered was waking up lying in Kyle's bed with a cold towel on my forehead and a sheet draped over my naked body. The camera was off, as was my fake mustache, and Kyle sat on his desk chair opposite the bed.

"Are you okay?"

"What happened?" I tried to sit up. The room spun like

Dorothy's house in the infamous twister, so I rested my head back on Kyle's pillow.

"You fainted," Kyle explained. "I couldn't call the dorm nurse, because she doesn't know about my...business. You can stay here as long as you need to."

"Thanks." I took in a few deep breaths and the room started to move slower, like in that Fred Astaire movie when Fred danced on the walls and the ceiling. "I'll be okay in a few minutes." *After the feeling of total humiliation wears off.* "I hope I'm not keeping you from a class."

Kyle shook his head and his long, dark hair brushed his face so reminiscent of his mother's. "No worries. I don't have a class for another hour." He smirked. "I know you don't have a class, since the Theatre Department has been shut down."

Butch Whopper bites the prairie dust. "How did you know?"

Kyle laughed benevolently. "My mom pointed you out to me in backstage photos from your shows over the years. She told me you are her favorite colleague in the Theatre Department."

I covered my face with my hands. "So why did you let me make a fool of myself?"

After handing me a bottle of water, Kyle said, "You were pretty good, Professor. You could have a career in porn."

I took a sip of water. "You bought the Butch Whopper routine?"

He laughed. "If Butch Whopper is any indication of your acting skills, you should stick to directing."

Ouch!

He explained, "I mean, you *sure as shootin'* have the equipment to be in porn, but you'd need to get over your stage fright, and you are a bit over the hill."

I'll register for social security once I can get of your bed.

Kyle shook my hand. "Hello, Professor Abbondanza, I'm Kyle Samson."

"Nice to meet you, Kyle." It was time to come clean. "Four of my colleagues have been murdered, including your father.

My boyfriend is the top suspect, according to the detectives assigned to the case. They've been interviewing people, taking fingerprints, looking for fibers no doubt, and they haven't come to any conclusions...except to shut down my department. I want to find the murderer, and find him fast, before he hurts anyone else, including your mother. Will you help me by answering a few questions?"

After moving his chair closer to the bed, Kyle added, "You promise me you won't tell the police or my mother about my little *business*, and I promise to answer as many of your questions as I can before the start of my next class. Deal?"

"Deal." The room rocked mildly as if I was a passenger on a cruise (meaning a boat).

Kyle leaned back against the wall with the front legs of his chair dangling in the air. "Fire away, Professor."

"Can I put my clothes on first? And can you destroy my audition tape?"

"You got it, Butch."

A few minutes later Kyle and I sat next to a floor to ceiling window in an unoccupied lounge in Kyle's dormitory. Since I was still in my cowboy outfit (with my hat on my lap), I was grateful when Kyle explained that the other students living in that wing were in classes, at the library, or in their rooms sleeping off the party from the night before. As we watched the snow falling over the low stone wall separating the college from the surrounding frozen lake and snow-capped mountains, we rested on overstuffed chairs while sipping too sweet hot chocolate from a vending machine nearby.

"You are certainly an industrious guy."

He looked at my cowboy outfit and raised his Styrofoam cup in my direction.

"Tell me about your childhood."

He laughed. "Should I lie down on the sofa over there?"

Thinking back to the debacle in Kyle's dorm room, I said, "I think there's been enough lying down for one day."

"True." He thought a moment then rolled his eyes as an entryway back in time. "I had a childhood filled with love and attention."

"From *both* your parents?"

Kyle took a sip of hot chocolate, which left a brown ring on his upper lip, reminding me of my long gone Butch Whopper mustache. "Professor, your question should be, what was my *dad's* childhood like?"

I nodded. "Okay."

Kyle looked out the window. "My father's early years consisted of living in a two-room apartment where the mice ate better than he did. Nighttime family activities included his father beating his mother…and beating him, that is until his father passed out from whatever booze he could steal. Since my dad was so poor, his clothes came from charities…stolen. Dad didn't have school supplies, and he never learned how to ride a bicycle or play sports. So the kids on the block bullied and beat him, often leaving him bleeding and crying in the gutter. My father learned early on how to lie, cheat, steal, and do whatever it took to stay alive long enough to get the hell out of there, which he did. When he was eighteen he stole his mother's jewelry and took a bus from Maine to Vermont, where he worked just about every type of job from toilet bowl cleaner to shoeshine boy to busboy while living in a room at the Y. Dad was smart enough to know the only way out was through education. So he worked his way through college and eventually graduate school."

I put my hand on his shoulder. "I think I understand."

"No, Professor, I don't think you do. See even after my father got his PHD, and came here as a college professor, he carried all that garbage from his past right along with him. He assumed that everyone was still out to get him. That the only way for him to stay alive was to get *them first*. That meant stealing grant money from the college, blackmailing the All College Promotion and Tenure Committee, and standing up to Wally Wanker when Professor Wanker was department head and didn't support Dad's tenure."

"But after your dad was tenured and moved from

Assistant to Associate and ultimately full Professor, why did he continue to...follow the old patterns?"

Kyle leaned forward in his chair and blinked away a tear. "Don't you see, it's all he knew? All of that rage, fear, I'll get you before you get me dysfunctional mentality had become totally ingrained in him. It had *become* him. So attacking his colleagues and trying to become department head was my father's way of becoming king of the hill so nobody could ever again try to throw him off the mountain."

From the mouths of babes. "You're a smart kid."

He laughed. "I'm a Psych minor. The Psychology Department has some amazing professors."

"Your father was an amazing scenic designer, and your mother is a first rate costume designer."

He nodded

A sip of hot chocolate went straight to a tooth cavity. "Were you upset when your parents split up?"

Kyle let out a heartbreaking snicker. "There were so many arguments. So much unhappiness between them."

"Why do you think that was?"

"As you know, my parents were total opposites. My mom is easy going, loyal, affectionate. She has certain...values. My dad was none of those things."

"But they had many things in common."

"Like what?"

I thought a moment. "You, the college, the world of academia, the field of theatre."

"That sounds more like the basis of a business partnership than a marriage, Professor."

I scratched my chest, which itched from razor burn. "Were you upset about your father's..."

"Indiscretions?"

"Yes."

A sad look filled his young face. "I knew my parents' marriage was in trouble. I actually was happy when they separated."

"Why didn't your parents get legally divorced?"

"Financial reasons. Their money was all tied up together."

And if they had gotten divorced, your mother would have no claim on your father's and his girlfriends' money now.

The itching moved downward, so with my hat on my lap I scratched unnoticed. "What did you think of your father's girlfriends?"

"Not too much." Kyle moved his long hair behind his ears, revealing the look of resentment on his face.

Trying not to sound like a reporter, I asked, "Can you be more specific?"

Kyle finished his drink and threw the cup into a nearby garbage bin. "As I'm sure you know, Loptu Lee was a total wack job, and Millie Rodriguez was my father's dishrag."

Joining him at the trash can, I asked, "Do you know that your father is the beneficiary in both of their wills?"

He nodded. "My mom told me."

"Do you also know that if their families don't contest their wills, you and your mother will inherit their money?"

"She mentioned something about that."

"How do you feel about that?"

He moved back to the seating area. "I'm not going to lie, Professor. I can use the money, just like any other student here with this insane tuition, not to mention the lab fees and the cost of textbooks."

Sitting again facing him, I said, "But your parents are professors here. You can go to Treemeadow with free tuition, and you can live with your mother off campus and not have to pay for room and board at the dorm."

He laughed bitterly. "No I can't."

"Why not?"

A look of rage overtook his young face. *Kyle is definitely David's son.* "My father wouldn't allow me to use the employee's family waiver. He said *he* had to work *his* way through college, and so do *I*."

My eyes flew out of my head like intergalactic spacecrafts in a mall movie. "Are you saying your father forced you to work to pay for your college tuition and dormitory room and board when you could have been a student here for free?"

He bit his lip, nearly drawing blood. "That's what I'm saying, Professor. Dad believed paying my own way would, *build needed character* in me. We had a huge argument about it. My mother took my side." He added resentfully, "As you can see, my mother and I lost. I will *never* forgive my father for that." Kyle added with a sarcastic laugh, "And he was the faculty advisor for the Christian Fellowship Club. So much for taking care of the poor and destitute. It's a good thing his graduate assistant took over the helm."

Based on Tyler's clothes and grooming habits, Tyler certainly looks like he understands the poor and destitute. "So you started your...*business*, which your father supported?"

After a glib laugh, Kyle responded, "Not in the beginning. But after Dad saw the potential for money coming in, his green eyes and controlling nature couldn't resist overseeing things."

I scratched at my shaved arms. "How do you keep the campus Security staff and the college's administration from finding out you are using college space and equipment for your...*private enterprise*?"

"My dad took care of that."

No doubt with bribes and/or pay offs. "And your mother never found out?"

"She heard about it, but I denied it." Kyle patted my shoulder. "And you promised me that you wouldn't tell her, Professor."

I nodded. "What made you think of starting an adult web site?"

"After the third girl in my dorm wing appeared in my bed at night, I thought, since everybody's banging the hell out of each other around here anyway, we might as well make some money out of it."

"Why did you enlist my theatre students as your actors?"

"People think adult films are about young people with good bodies getting into various sexual positions."

"Aren't they?"

Kyle answered like a bank C.E.O. addressing his Board of Directors. "Sexual arousal isn't about body parts. It's about the *libido*. To get into the brains of viewers, films need to have characters who make real connections, and experience real emotions. Your theatre students understood that and brought my films to a higher level."

Especially since three of them have the hots for the fourth.

"As acting students, they understand about relationships, role play, dominance, passivity, allure, teasing, and eventually succumbing to their innate carnal desires."

Noah will be thrilled to know he prepared his acting students for your porn movies!

"Besides, the theatre students need money for their tuition."

"Kyle, with your father deceased, who is acting as your producer and distributor now?"

Kyle glanced at his watch. "Faith O'Riley."

"The name sounds familiar."

"It should. She's a Screenwriting professor in the Film Department here at Treemeadow."

That peaked my interest. "How did Professor O'Riley come onboard?"

He rose and used a rubber band from his pocket to tie his hair in a ponytail. "Faith came along courtesy of Dad."

I stood to meet his eyes. "I don't understand."

"Faith was Dad's latest squeeze...after he dumped Millie."

"I thought—"

"Dad told me Millie got too needy. So after he convinced her to have the abortion, he moved on to Faith, who is younger and more...independent."

Blocking his path back to his dorm room, I asked, "When did Faith O'Riley become your producer?"

"Shortly before Dad died, Faith came to my dorm room to talk to me about a screenplay I wrote for her class. I told her I appreciated her ideas on the script. One thing led to another, and she told me she knew about my film company...from my Dad. First I panicked, but Faith assured me that she was okay with it. To my surprise, she asked me if she could replace Dad as producer and distributor of the company."

"For what reason?"

"She said things between her and Dad were getting rocky. She blamed Loptu and Millie for trying to hold onto him. She also said she needed the money."

"Why?"

He shrugged his broad shoulders. "Don't we all need money?"

Kyle took a few more steps, and I again blocked his path. "How are things working out with Faith O'Riley replacing your father?"

"Okay. She's been doing the business end, and I've been taking care of the artistic side." Unleashing a lascivious grin, Kyle added, "I'm meeting with her tonight as usual...in my bed. Take care, Professor. Remember your promise."

I stared at Kyle's wide back and bouncing ponytail as his long legs walked him back to his dorm room. While leaving the dormitory hallway, I passed an open Housekeeping supply cabinet laden with pillows, blankets, sheets, cleaning products, and a large box of rat poison.

Chapter Ten

After Butch Whopper's short-lived career ended, Noah met me outside of Kyle's dormitory, where Noah had dropped me off earlier. Upon looking at my dejected face, Noah threw a coat over me, and drove me back to *our* house. My heart was in my mouth as Noah sped along the narrow, winding, icy road hovering over snow-covered twin peaks, as he looked at me, asking frantically, "So what happened?"

Once I convinced Noah to watch the road, and slow down to twenty miles per hour over the speed limit, I caught him up on my foray into porn stardom.

"I can't believe Kyle saw through your disguise."

"Me, too." I threw the fake mustache out the car window.

Stealing glances at me as he passed a truck, Noah said, "It's exciting that Kyle thought you could have a future in porn."

"In case I want to start a new career?" I moved his hand from my knee back to the steering wheel.

"I just think you are incredibly hot, and I'm glad Kyle thinks so too…unless he's gay then I'll scratch his eyes out."

After scratching my razor burned legs, I responded, "Kyle is hardly gay. He is having an affair with Faith O'Riley who teaches in the Film Department, who by the way was his father's ex-girlfriend."

Noah looked at me aghast. As I pushed his chin to face forward, he said, "I thought *Millie* was David's ex-girlfriend."

"It seems that we can add Professor O'Riley to the list of David's conquests. And my chest itches."

Noah scratched my chest for me. I moved his hand back onto the steering wheel, as he asked, "What was Kyle's take

137

on the murder victims?"

"He loved his father...sort of. And he hated Wally for trying to deny David's tenure years back, and Loptu and Millie for being...Loptu and Millie."

After a long whistle, Noah said, "Well, Kyle might not have liked Loptu and Millie, but he certainly likes his father's last girlfriend."

I corrected him. *I have to stop doing this!* "Professor O'Riley is also Kyle's current porn movie producer and distributor."

"What a tangled web we weave." Noah sped around a frightened deer.

"Mr. Magoo, can you please slow down and watch the road, so we stay alive long enough to catch the killer?"

"You got it, honey."

He called me honey!

Noah turned down a local side street and we drove (thankfully) slowly past homes laden with decorated snowmen, cottony smoke coming from chubby chimneys, and porch swings rocking mounds of snow.

As Noah rounded the turn to the house, he asked, "Do you think Kyle is our murderer?"

"Financial gain and revenge are strong motives. And as a dorm student Kyle has access to college buildings, thereby college offices. He had visited Millie at home in the past, so she would have opened her door to Kyle that night." I added, "And there's the thing about the rat poison."

"Kyle had rat poison?"

"It was in the supply closet in Kyle's dorm wing."

Noah's eyes bulged out of his head. "The plot thickens!"

A few minutes later, sans clothing, Noah and I were submerged in strawberry scented bubbles in my claw foot tub. Sitting behind me, Noah massaged the tension from my shoulders and back muscles while we sipped three-berry herbal tea. Pressing my back into Noah's firm pectoral muscles, I melted into his soft, sensual touch. Tantalizingly illuminated by the vanilla scented candles surrounding us, Noah came to a sudden conclusion. "Nicky, Faith O'Riley could be the key to the entire mystery."

I turned to face Noah, splashing sudsy water onto the tile floor. "How do you mean?"

As if a five-year-old teaching a three-year-old how to tie his shoe, Noah answered, "Think about it, Nicky. Faith O'Riley was dating David, but she switched teams to Kyle and then replaced David as Kyle's producer. Becoming the producer of a lucrative business will bring her some nice money. Plus, if she has designs on marrying Kyle, killing David, Loptu, and Millie would be another cash cow for our colleague from the Film Department."

I put my arms around Noah and pressed our bodies together. "But where does Wally fit into the Faith O'Riley equation?"

"That's what we have to find out." He kissed the suds on my chin. "You have to call Professor O'Riley."

After noticing our rock-hard penises waving in the water below, I grinned like a teenager setting fire to his virgin card. "Yes, I'll call her. In about a half hour."

Noah and I kissed, hugged, caressed, and added a lot more foam to the bath water. Once we were dried off and in our sky-blue (Noah) and burgundy (me) terrycloth bathrobes, we sat in the kitchen breakfast nook and I phoned Faith O'Riley.

Catching the Screenwriting professor just before she was about to leave her office for the day, I introduced myself and asked to speak to her regarding the murders at the college. Professor O'Riley told me in no uncertain terms that she had already spoken to Detective Manuello and Detective Dickerson, and she had no intention of talking to me. When I told Ms. O'Riley that I knew about her affair with a student in her program, the dial tone at the other end of the line proved she meant business.

* * *

Early the next morning with my eyes glued shut from sleep, Noah sat up next to me in bed shaking my shoulders. "Nicky!

Nicky, are you up?"

Feeling like a coma victim taken off life support, I asked, "What's wrong?" I yawned.

"I have a plan."

After scratching my legs from the lingering razor burn, I asked, "Give me a heart attack?"

"I know how we can reach Faith O'Riley."

I peeled my eyes open then shielded them from the beaming Tiffany lamp on the night table. "I tried calling Professor O'Riley yesterday, Noah. Don't you remember? She wouldn't talk to me. I doubt she'll talk to you either."

Noah posed theatrically against the carved wooden headboard, and said like a Shakespearian actor, "But Professor O'Riley will talk to *Reggie McCallister.*"

Hiding under my pillow, I asked, "Do I have to be a porn star again?"

He let out a theatrical chortle. "Quite the contrary, Nicky. The star has taken to his bed." Noah pointed to himself proudly. "So the understudy must go on."

With that Noah draped his robe around his shoulders, sauntered over to the Victorian vanity, and phoned our allusive film professor.

"Ms. O'Riley, Reggie McCallister here from 'Man Muscle Mania to the Max Magazine.'" *How did he say that so early in the morning?* "Dear heart, I am in Vermont on a little skiing vacation with a few blokes, and I would like to interview *you* regarding your *up and coming* — pardon the pun — film company, As Young as You F___ Productions." *Why is he talking with a British accent?* "I read *all* about your novice company on your charming little web site." *Oh brother!* "Yes, 'Man Muscle Mania to the Max Magazine' has the *largest* readership of any all-male magazine and web site in the country, actually in the *world*!" He snickered affectedly. "Men who get off, get *us*, get it?" *Heaven help us!* "Yes, darling, I am *very* aware that all-male fare is only *part* of your scintillating film offerings." *Thanks to the two leading men of my play.* "I would simply *adore* taking you to lunch today to hear *all* about that part…of your company…and *all* about your latest man on man films." *If she buys this act, I have a solid gold bridge to sell her.* "No, darling, I wish I could, but I will be gone tomorrow. Back to London on the bloody red eye, love. So it absolutely *has* to be today, or I am afraid you will lose the interview…*and* the promotion for your company, dear one." *He sounds like Captain Hook on speed.* "Perfect! Meet me at one o'clock at the Food Fantasia on Treemeadow Street. You will know me, lovey, since I am absolutely gorgeous!" *Gorgeous, but insane.* "See you then, love bug. Cheers!"

With that, the interview was sealed, and Reggie McCallister, porn promoter, was born.

That afternoon Noah, rather Reggie McCallister, sat opposite Professor Faith O'Riley in the corner of the Food Fantasia restaurant two blocks away from the college. Courtesy of our Theatre Department's Costume Shop, Noah, I mean Reggie, wore a long black coat, black beret, yellow shirt, purple ascot, red pants, and purple boots. By contrast, the film professor, though about Noah's *young* age, wore a gray trench coat over a navy pants suit with a white blouse and pearl drop gold necklace. Her long chestnut hair was twisted into a bun, and pearl drop gold earrings hung from her delicate earlobes, which were the only delicate thing about her.

Saying Professor O'Riley seemed a tad ambitious was like saying right-wing talk radio had a bit of an agenda. With squinting dark eyes, a long narrow nose, thin lips, a pointy chin, and an annoying sniffling habit, Faith O'Riley needed only a big black hat and a facial wart to be ready for Halloween.

I sat inconspicuously eavesdropping at a table behind them, wearing all black, hopelessly lost in the newspaper that covered my face — except for my eyes and ears.

Noah removed the tip of his ascot from inside his mouth, and said to Professor O'Riley, "Thank you for taking the time for our little interview, love. I know you will be *most* pleased with the result."

After looking around the room to make sure there were no recognizable faces from the college, Faith asked sotto voce (but loud enough for me to hear by picking up my dropped fork), "Mr. McCallister, how did you know where to find me? Our company's web site doesn't mention me or the college by name?"

Reggie, rather Noah, thought fast, no doubt grateful for his years of training in improvisational theatre. "Please call me, Reggie, dear heart. *Everyone* does, except my mum who calls me, well, that language might cause even a producer of porn to blush." After unleashing a nasal laugh to the second balcony—if the restaurant had balconies, Noah appeared to have his answer. "Dear one, someone named David Samson emailed me a while back stating that he and his son, Kyle I believe, were embarking on a new career with a web site touting adult films for discerning viewers of both the gay and straight varieties. Mr. Samson asked if my magazine and web site might be of some assistance in publicizing his new blue venture. To be perfectly frank, darling, I had forgotten all about Mr. Samson's email until three blokes who I regularly…am *associated* with invited me to a *lovely* little cabin in Vermont quite near the college." After refilling his diaphragm with air, Noah continued his performance by flailing his arms with such fervor that Faith moved her water glass to escape its demise. "And, precious, the *moment* I arrived in your snowdrift of a town, I recalled Mr. Samson's email, located it in the delete column on my laptop, and phoned Mr. Samson's office. The secretary who answered the phone, a woman named Shayla I believe, informed me that Mr. Samson had sadly gone on to meet his maker. Discouraged but never dismayed, I asked Madame Shayla for Kyle Samson's phone number, upon which my call was forwarded to a dormitory at your alluring axle of academia."

He should get a Tony Award for this performance, or have his Actors Equity card revoked.

Primping the wide collar of his lemon-yellow shirt, Noah continued as if reciting a soliloquy from the Bard at the Globe

Theatre. "And, dear heart, when I phoned the deceased's son, young Mr. Samson referred me to *you*. And here we are, having *come*, you should pardon the expression, *face to face*."

With an understandably skeptical look on her stern face, Faith asked, "And how exactly will you be publicizing my company?"

After spewing out another guffaw that nearly cracked the mirror on the wall behind them, Noah waved a delicate finger in her direction. "Now, now honey bunny, don't be coy with me. As a successful producer of adult celluloid, you are *certainly* well aware of 'Muscle Mania to the Max Magazine' and web site, and how an article from us could catapult your films and ricochet big bucks for you! If I so much as mention you on our bountiful blog, or teasingly tweet your company name, your sales will shoot, pardon the word, through the stratosphere."

"I did a computer search on your web site and came up empty."

"Oh, darling, I forgot to mention, our web site is temporarily down, but it will be *back up*, pardon the pun, later this afternoon."

I held my breath.

Thankfully greed overtook sense as Faith nodded, and said, "Mr. McCallister—"

He raised a hand as if trying to stop an overflowing dam with orphans in its path. "Please, call me Reggie."

"Reggie—"

He blew her a stagey kiss. "Call me Reg."

Oh, brother.

"Reg, please don't mention anything about the college in your article. I am Professor of Screenwriting at Treemeadow, but this business is a *totally* separate entity and *must* remain so."

Right, using the college's cameras, lighting equipment, editing equipment, computers, locations — and students!

Noah clutched at his heart like the dying swan in *Swan Lake*. "Oh, dear heart, you wound me to the core. I would never ever *ever* breathe a word to my millions of readers about your company's *or your* affiliation with Treemeadow College."

Millions of readers?

Faith's shoulders dropped down to her ears. After a few irritating sniffs, she replied tensely, "Thank you. I make it a rule to keep the various facets of my life separate from one another."

Yeah, like being Kyle's producer, professor, and paramour. (Try saying that three times fast.)

Reg continued grandly. "Oh course, darling. I too am *fanatical* about not mixing business with pleasure. And I am the epitome of discretion." Still in character (I hope), Noah salivated over the busboy cleaning the next table.

Faith rubbed her nose with her napkin, and said in producer mode, "With the change in producers, and with our fast-growing stock of films, As Young As You F___ Productions could certainly use the publicity."

He spread his arms like a musical comedy star belting an elongated final high C. "Of course, dumpling. That is why I am here! But let us order our delectable ditties first."

We all ordered and had our lunches served (Noah Cobb salad, Faith lobster salad, and me chicken Caesar salad with extra croutons to drop/retrieve/listen). Faith, between annoying sniffs, spoke proudly about Kyle's "amazing gifts" as a filmmaker, leaving out the fact that she had experienced Kyle's other *amazing gifts* in his dorm room. She next went through their inventory of films, highlighting the movies starring my students, Paul and Ricky: *Study Buddies, Top of the Class, Muscles 101,* and *Cafeteria: Light Meat or Dark Meat?*

Remembering his salad wasn't prop food, Noah took a bite then rolled his eyes around in his head like a loading computer. "Ah! This is the best Cobb salad I have *ever* had north of San Francisco."

Faith moved her lobster around her plate with her fork but never took a bite. Given her constant sniffing, I wondered if she might inhale the food through her nose.

After pretending to take copious notes on his napkin about Faith's company, Noah finally turned his, and Faith's, attention to the murders. Taking her hand in his, he said, "You know, love muffin, given the unfortunate death of your company's former producer/distributor and your director's father, you are to be commended for so successfully stepping in and taking control of the company."

Luckily she seemed to buy it. Faith cracked a half smile for the first time all afternoon. "Thank you, Reg."

Moving their water glasses aside, Noah ordered a glass of white wine for Faith and a carrot ginger juice for himself, no doubt with the motivation of loosening her tongue and keeping his in his head.

After they sipped their drinks, Noah pounded his hand on the table like a defense attorney making closing arguments in a television movie. "I can only imagine how *gravely* traumatic his father's death must have been for poor, *young* Kyle." He added as if an afterthought, "And for *you.*"

Squirming in her seat and sniffing more than a police dog at a drug raid, Faith replied with artificial melancholy, "David was a wonderful man who will be missed." She continued mid sniff. "Many people at the college loved him dearly."

Sure, Ariella, Loptu, Millie, and you until you dumped him for his son!

Noah covered his face with his napkin a la Madame Butterfly. "How did David die, pudding pop? I hope it wasn't too *gruesome.*"

The wine seemed to be working as Faith sat back in her chair and took in a deep breath. "The whole story is in the local papers, Reg. It closed down the Theatre Department at the college."

He raised a knuckle to his mouth and bit on it. "Pray tell me, as a non-native of Treemeadow!"

After finishing her drink, Faith finished her story. "David was murdered, along with three of his colleagues in the Theatre Department. The murderer is still at lodge."

Noah threw his arms around her, nearly falling off his chair. "You poor, dear darling. How *horrible*. How *abominable*. How *barbaric*."

Once the waiter brought a refill for Faith, she took a few sips, and replied, "Yes, it has everyone on campus on edge, including *me*."

"Well, no wonder, cumquat. You were David's business partner after all."

She shook her head and sniffed at the same time. "No, I came on board as producer and distributor *after* David had departed."

Not according to Kyle. Too bad she wasn't eating baloney.

Noah patted her hand in commiseration. "But, butterball, you and David Samson were colleagues at the same college. You *must* have had...*affection* for one another?"

"At one time." Faith finished her drink and Noah briskly ordered a third.

Noah reeled her in like a fisherman with a prized catch. "Of course this is one hundred percent completely and totally off the record, sweet pea, but I'm guessing that you and David were, how should we say, *coeds?*"

After practically swallowing her drink down in one gulp then burping and sniffing (at the same time), Faith loosened the collar of her blouse. "David and I were...together for a while."

Noah's eyes lit up like bonfires. "And did David's death take you away from the arms of your one true love?"

She laughed and sniffed at the same time. "Not exactly." Faith seemed to have a moment of lucidity. "What does this have to do with your story on As Young as you F___ Productions?"

Thinking fast, Noah responded, "Baby breath, our business is *all* about *love*. How can we sell love to others, if we have never experienced it ourselves?" He winked at her. "And believe me, I have certainly *experienced* it."

Faith summoned the waiter for a fourth drink and polished it off before he left the table.

Reg was back with a flourish of his ascot. "So please don't keep me in suspense a moment longer, cream puff. Do tell what happened between you and David...prior to his *unfortunate exit.*"

"What *happened*, Reg, was David's wife. That bitch was jealous of me."

Ariella, jealous?

Scratching his head, or rather his beret, Noah responded, "But wouldn't most wives be jealous of their husband's girlfriend?"

Faith's voice, and sniffs, grew louder and more strident. "David and his wife were separated. She said she was done with him. Then she bad-mouthed Loptu then Millie then me to David."

After the waiter brought Faith's fifth drink, Noah said in a mock effort to understand, "Are Loptu and Millie David's past girlfriends?"

"You mean his past bitches?" With her fifth glass of wine history, Faith unbuttoned her blouse, and shouted to the waiter, "Waiter, give me another bitch, I mean, another glass of white!" Then she turned back to Noah, and said, "Millie and Loptu were jealous of me too. They told David that I was a cocaine addicted drunk."

Hence the sniffing and guzzling wine.

Noah as Reg gasped in horror. "How utterly *reprehensible.*"

Faith's tongue was looser than a right-wing politician in the back room of a gay bar. "And David *believed* them! He told me to get off cocaine, or it would be over between us."

Noah cried on cue into his napkin. "You poor, poor darling."

Clenching her jaw between two sniffs, Faith said, "I'm glad they're all dead."

Noah parched his lips like a silent film star. "Who is all dead?"

"David, Loptu, and Millie...and that creep Wally."

Noah let the waterworks go. "What did this elderly Wally do to *you*, dear one?"

She asked between sniffs, "How did you know Wally was old?"

Counting on the effects of the wine, Noah responded, "The name, doodle. What young person would be called Wally, except on the telly?"

She nodded with glazed over eyes. "Wally was this dinosaur of a retired guy in the Theatre Department who spied on David. After finding David and me...together, the old pig came on to me in my office at the college, telling me if I didn't put out for him, he would tell everyone on campus about David and me...and about the film company. I told Wally Wanker to stick his withered sausage up his ancient ass."

Between dramatic sobs, Noah said, "Oh, how *horrible* for you. How horribly horrible."

Her head bobbed, and her eyes crossed between sniffs.

Noah held on like a dog with a roast beef. "So you did what any woman with a weapon would do in your position—you *killed* them all."

Shaking herself back into coherency, Faith responded, "I didn't kill anybody. I was a basket case."

"Of course you were, dear breath. And during your *Nightmare on Treemeadow Street*, did you have *anyone* who could stand by your side through all of this *horrendously* unfair assassination of your character!"

"Kyle. Only Kyle stood by me. So I stood by *him*." Faith's face hardened like cement.

After giving her a stagey hug, Noah said conspiratorially, "So you, lonely, abused, downtrodden darling ended the cycle of abuse by David, and you sought solace, protection, and *love* in the arms of the only man on this campus, the only man in this town who stood up to the ridicule that wounded you so miserably. The ridicule from his mother, his father, his father's ex-colleague, and his father's ex-girlfriends."

"Somebody finally understands!" Faith cried on Noah's shoulder.

Noah patted her back and winked at me. "Sugarplum, how

exactly did Kyle protect you from these *vicious* monsters?"

Faith looked at Noah through narrow eyes. "I don't know if I can trust you."

"Daffodil, you not only have Kyle as your protector, now you also have *me*...for the rest of the afternoon."

After blowing her nose into her napkin, Faith took Noah's hand. "Thank you, Reg."

He smiled broadly. "Two men are better than one."

Just like in your porn movies.

Between hiccups and sniffs, Faith corrected Noah. "Actually, I have three men to protect me."

Noah clapped his hands together like a seal in a theme park show. "Hooray! That is *wonderful*, dumpling. And who pray tell is the third man in the trinity?"

Faith wiped the mascara from her cheeks with her napkin. "My half-sister teaches at the college too...in the Theatre Department. Well, now after the sex change operation, he's my brother."

After Noah's gasp nearly sent the tablecloth to the floor, Faith O'Riley passed out on the table.

CHAPTER ELEVEN

That night Reggie and Butch, I mean Noah and I made passionate love, leaving all four of us exhausted but too stimulated to sleep. Sitting up in bed with my laptop hugging my knees and Noah hugging my torso, I emailed an invitation to my show's cast and crew members to come to my house the following evening for a production meeting and a line-through of the play.

By the time I pressed send, Noah was lightly snoring on my stomach. I was still too charged up to sleep. So I started a new computer file called, Suspects and Motives. As thoughts about the murders filled my head like jelly beans in a contest jar, I typed faster than a secretary at 4:55 pm. Finally my head dropped over the computer and I entered sleep land.

* * *

Noah and I woke the next morning and bypassed the online morning newspapers for my computerized notes. Sitting up shoulder to shoulder in bed with the sun from the windows illuminating the screen, we reviewed my file:

SUSPECTS AND MOTIVES by Nicky, rather Sherlock

Ariella: 1) To get David's, Loptu's, and Millie's money. 2) To take revenge on David and his girlfriends for ending her marriage. 3) To take revenge on Wally for not supporting David's past tenure.

Kyle: 1) Same as 1-3 above. 2) To replace David with Faith as his producer/film distributor. 3) To take revenge on Wally for blackmailing Faith.

Faith: 1) Same as 2 & 3 above. 2) To use her producer income to feed her cocaine habit. 3) To take a younger man, Kyle, as her lover.

Jackson: 1) To stop David and Wally from spreading the word about his secret past as Jillson. 2) To take revenge on Loptu and Millie for going with David. 3) To protect his sister, Faith, from David, Loptu, Millie, and Wally.

Scotty: 1) To take over Millie's classes, faculty committee, and student club.

Tyler: 1) To take over David's classes, faculty committee, and student club. 2) To end David's criticisms of him.

Martin: 1) To stop David from running for department head and blocking Noah's tenure. 2) To stop David from stealing college grant money, 3) To stop Loptu and Millie from supporting David for department head. 4) To stop Wally from saying, "When I was department head..."

As we ate breakfast in the kitchen nook, I couldn't help thinking I was missing something right under my nose, and it wasn't the blueberry buckwheat pancakes smothered in maple syrup that Noah had served us. That feeling haunted me as I took my vitamins then worked out at the campus gym.

I arrived back home sweaty but still in the dark about what I was missing. After a quick shower (together), Noah and I prepared hummus, crudités, sweet potato wedges, salmon balls, a fruit plate, and hot mulled apple cider for my meeting. As I filled a bowl with trail mix, I reminded Noah it was off limits to him due to his nut allergy. In thanks, he patted my nuts. As we balled the last melon (no pun intended), Ariella appeared on our (I love saying *our*!) wraparound porch dressed in her usual all black Morticia Adams attire. We were all happy to see that the press was no longer stationed at my door.

After hanging her black cape on the coat rack in the hallway, Ariella helped us set up the buffet on the dining room table and move the dining room chairs into the front and back parlors. After Ariella wedged the last chair between the sofa and fireplace in the back parlor, she plopped onto the sofa in exhaustion. Noah turned on lights all over the downstairs then went upstairs to change his clothes in *our* (again!) bedroom. I stuffed an almond from the trail mix into my mouth then lit a fire in the back parlor, forgetting Ariella was there.

Rubbing her bare feet then wiggling them in the direction of the fire, Ariella said, "I'm so happy for you and Noah. I always thought you two would make a great couple...and I was right!"

I giggled like a teenager holding a condom at a pharmacy counter. "Thanks. We're really happy."

"I can tell." Ariella took snapshots out of her purse and waved them at me. "I came early to show you these. Paul's new cape looks terrific on him, and it flows perfectly when he turns. I can't wait to see it under the lights when we get back into the theatre."

I looked at the pictures of Paul posing like a male model in his new costume. "Very nice." *Maybe Paul can take it off in Kyle's next porn flick.*

I stoked the fire then checked myself out in the mirror above the mantel. *I definitely look better without a mustache.*

Ariella said nonchalantly, "I bumped into Detective Manuello when I was leaving the Costume Shop yesterday."

I placed another log on the fire. "Did he mention anything about the murders?"

Her face, the little I could see of it inside her long, black hair, grew serious. "Manuello said they are closing in on a suspect, but he didn't say who."

"Did he scold you for being there?"

"No. He was non-committal about when we can come back, but he was very nice to me."

After jumping onto the sofa and landing nose to nose with Ariella, I asked, "Did he come on to you?"

She slapped my knee. "Behave yourself, Nicky. He was

just being friendly."

"You may have caught the attention of the senior Detective Manuello, but the novice Detective Dickerson came on to *me*."

"I gather you turned him down?"

I nodded. "Flat as a pancake. Noah is much more my cup of hunk."

Noah shouted from upstairs, "I agree!" *Ah, the thin walls of a Victorian home.*

"You're single now, Ariella. Granted Manuello is an overweight, incompetent, married—"

"Divorced."

My eyes widened. "Ah, you found that out, did you?"

Her white face turned pink. "Jose might have mentioned it."

"Jose, huh?"

"When you get to know him, he's a nice guy."

We giggled like schoolgirls.

"Well, you could do a lot worse than Manuello." *Actually you did worse with David.*

She hit me harder. "I've already been down that road, pal, with an older guy who wanted me." Ariella raised her eyes like a psychic at a carnival booth. "Thankfully it was a *long* time ago."

I rubbed my sore knee. "Do tell."

With a look on her face that said, 'I know you'll drag this out of me eventually,' Ariella said, "It was Wally Wanker, back when David was up for tenure."

The pieces came together in my mind like a child's jigsaw puzzle. "Wally blackmailed you, didn't he? He wanted sex with you in return for supporting David's tenure."

Ariella was clearly surprised. "How did you know?"

"It seems to fit the pattern around here." I took her hand. It was iced cold. "Ariella, what did you do when Wally came on to you back then?"

She chortled bitterly. "Obviously I turned him down...and told him off. As you know, David was quite capable of illegally working the system to secure his tenure."

"I spoke with Kyle yesterday in the Film Department."

"I'm glad he's getting back to his studies and his filmmaking. Even though his father was no Father of the Year...or Husband of the Year, David's death hit Kyle pretty hard."

Given Kyle's line of work, hard is the operative word. "Kyle seems to be...adapting quite well. He's a smart, mature kid."

She nodded. "Sometimes it feels like he's the parent and I'm the child."

I squeezed her hand. "Ariella, I also...overheard someone speaking with Faith O'Riley."

Taking her hand out of mine, Ariella said disgustedly, "Another one of David's mistakes."

Salivating on my lime fleece shirt, I tried to ask casually, "Were you jealous of David's girlfriends?"

"Jealous? Are you kidding me!" She waved her arms like the conductor of a rock opera. "Loptu had a split personality. Millie was a masochist. Faith is a cocaine addict. I would think that even David could have done better than them." She put her shoes back on. "Believe me, when David first cheated on me, I was devastated. I cried for weeks. I even thought about ending it all. But then I realized that I couldn't change David, and he couldn't change me. I decided it was time to move on. Besides, I have my job and my son to keep me occupied." Sounding like a country western singer, Ariella added trying to convince herself more than me, "I don't need a man in my life."

I rested my elbow on the arm of the sofa. "Do you know that Faith and Kyle are involved *together* in a...film project?"

Avoiding my eyes, she responded, "That makes sense since she's his professor."

"Ariella, does Kyle ever talk about Faith to you."

Her eyes moved to one side like a broken pendulum. "I don't think so."

She needs to take a crash course in acting with Noah. "Now that David has passed away, why doesn't Kyle move back home with you, and accept the college's offer of free tuition as a professor's son?"

"This is his last semester." She added proudly, "He's already paid his tuition and room and board. Plus, I think he likes living in the dorm."

I think I know why.

Ariella said, "Kyle has made his own way at Treemeadow." She added with a content smile, "Like father, like son."

Exactly.

"Have no fear, your graduate assistant is here!" Since I had left the door unlocked after Ariella's entrance, Scotty had let himself in and stood in the front parlor wearing his usual winter garb—pink tank top, denim shorts, work boots, and a seductive smile.

I walked over to him. "Aren't you cold, Scotty?"

As he pointed to his thin overcoat hanging on the coat rack in the hall, Scotty flexed his shoulder, pectoral, and bicep muscles. "My coat keeps my body warm, but my friends keep *my heart* warm."

Noah came down the long, flared staircase looking, as Reg would say, *fetchingly* in an indigo ribbed sweater, tight black slacks, and black loafers with no socks. I wanted to pick him up over my shoulder, carry him back up the stairs, and have my way with him. *All in due time.*

After wrapping his arm around my waist, Noah said to Scotty, "Our nights have gotten much hotter since I moved in here with Nicky."

Scotty gasped like a boxer suffering a one-two punch in the gut. "I didn't realize that you two were...*cohabitating.*" He got his breath back, unfortunately. "I didn't know that you liked leftovers, Nicky, especially *mine.*"

Before I could knock Scotty into the next state, Ariella put her arms around Noah and me, and said, "Where have *you* been, Scotty? These two guys have been nuts about each other for years. It was only a matter of time before they got together. And it couldn't happen to two nicer guys."

"Here come the grooms!" After belting out his little ditty,

Jackson threw his coat on the coat rack, kissed both Noah and me on the cheek, and shouted, "Mazel tov to you both!"

Ariella asked, "Are you Jewish?"

Jackson replied, "Only when I want a good seat in a Jewish deli."

After laughing so hard he nearly ruptured a windpipe, Scotty linked his short muscular arm through Jackson's lengthy graceful one. "You are such a riot."

Noah whispered in my ear, "Looks like I'm safe tonight."

After nibbling Noah's neck, I replied, "Don't count on it."

Focusing on Jackson like he was the only one in the room, Scotty said, "I love your white sweater, Jackson. It goes so *sexily* with your dark complexion. What material is it?"

"Cotton," replied Jackson with a shrug in my direction.

Scotty was not to be put off. "You *always* look terrific in your clothes." He snuggled up to Jackson's long, lean body. "I wonder what you look like with them *off*."

You may be surprised, Scotty.

We heard someone new enter the room and all turned to look at Tyler. David's graduate assistant seemed like a teenager whose parents had locked him out of the house past curfew. His eyes were red and swollen, and his long hair was even more unkempt than usual. The gloomy pout on his rugged face matched the worn, drab coat on his short, stocky body. As he hung up his coat, I noticed he was wearing his techie clothes, even though we weren't in the theatre. As usual his gold cross dangled from his neck, and his arms displayed a creative multitude of words and pictures.

I waved him into the front parlor. "Are you all right?"

He replied unconvincingly, "I'm okay," then he raised a sandpaper rough hand to wipe a tear off his unshaven cheek.

Ariella moved to Tyler's side and put her arm around him. "What's wrong?"

Dropping the stoic act, Tyler sat on the sofa with his head in his hands. "Everything. Everything is wrong."

We all gathered around him like birds to a carcass.

Tyler managed a stiff upper lip. "I'm sorry. I know this is

a production meeting. Let's go over the set, light, sound, and film projection cues for the show."

After sitting next to him and placing my hand on his oil-stained shoulder, I said soothingly, "The meeting can wait. Tell us why you are so upset."

Noah sat on Tyler's other side. "We want to help."

Jackson said compassionately, "Let it out."

Joining Jackson on the loveseat, Scotty said, "Show Tyler how to let it all hang out, Jackson." After Jackson poked him in the side, Scotty said, "I mean, what's wrong?"

Wiping a tear off his chin with his massive shoulder, Tyler said, "I'm going crazy. I can't stand it any longer."

"You mean having a murderer loose among us?" asked Ariella.

Tyler nodded. "David, Wally, Loptu, and Millie, their lives were taken...just like that!" He snapped his thick fingers and the sound echoed eerily through the front parlor. "I'm afraid that this is God's will...God's punishment for the things they did. I feel so sorry for each one of them." His dark eyes filled with fear. "And *any* one of *us* could be next!"

Who said gruff techies don't have big hearts? I put my arm around his leviathan shoulders. "What has happened is terrible. We're all concerned."

Scotty looked up at Jackson, and said, "I'm so scared, I don't want to sleep *alone* tonight."

Sitting opposite Tyler on a wingback chair covered with a rose pattern fabric, Ariella took his hand. "All of us are frightened and concerned about the future."

Tyler wiped his eyes on a dirty handkerchief. "That's just it. Whenever I'm upset, I throw myself into my work." He thought a moment. "I throw myself into my work when I'm not upset too." Then he looked at me like a kid begging to go to the beach. "It's killing me, Nicky, not being able to go into the theatre and refocus lights, test sound cues, touch up the paint on set pieces, or just...tinker. I feel like a caged animal. I'm really losing it. I won't make it much longer!"

They say, theatre is therapy. "Tyler, Ariella talked to

Detective Manuello." *And he tried to pick her up.* "Manuello said they are close to making an arrest."

Tyler put his now dirty *and* wet handkerchief back inside his overall's pocket. "Who are they arresting?"

"I don't know." Ariella looked at Tyler affectionately. "But I'm sure this nightmare will be over soon, and we will all be back to teaching our classes."

"And putting on the *show!*" Noah added like the star of a 1940's movie musical.

Jackson said warmly, "Tyler, soon you'll be teaching David's Technical Theatre classes again, serving on his faculty committee, and advising his student club."

Looking like a Christian martyr, Tyler responded, "The kids in the Christian Fellowship Club have been so upset. They've been on a prayer vigil since David's funeral."

Scotty tucked his shoulder under Jackson's, and said, "The Forensics students are performing a non-religious reader's theatre piece about loss. They're dedicating it to Millie."

As a true Unitarian, Ariella said, "Both groups of kids are terrific. This has been hard for us, but I think in some ways it has been even harder for our students. We've lost our colleagues and friends, but *they've* lost their teachers and mentors."

"I can't wait to get back to teaching Millie's Voice and Diction classes," said Scotty possessively — of the classes and of Jackson. "I could go on teaching her classes *forever.*"

I'm sure.

Noah said, "We *all* miss our classes, and our students."

In between their stints as porn stars.

Jackson and Ariella agreed.

I stood up. "All right, crew, let's all go get some drinks and snacks in the dining room then come back here to go over the logistics of our show's sets, props, lighting, sound, film projections, costumes, and movement choreography."

As my production team filled their plates with food and filled their minds with more worries about the murders, I cornered Jackson in the butler's pantry. (Unfortunately I don't have a butler, just his pantry.) The under-cabinet lighting gave Jackson's dark, smooth skin a radiant glow. *Or is the radiance a result of Scotty's interest in him?* "Jackson, I couldn't help but notice that my graduate assistant seems quite taken with you."

His long, delicate fingers rested his plate on the countertop then Jackson took a sip of hot cider. "Scotty appears to be a handful."

"He seems to really like you."

Jackson's small features expanded into a shrewd expression. "He's adorable, but Scotty's too young and too wild for someone who has been through what I've been through."

I winked. "Scotty may be a welcome diversion for you. And you may be just the guy to tame him."

"When our department reopens, I'll get the whip from the prop closet." Jackson smiled and headed back to the dining room.

"I ran into Faith O'Riley yesterday."

Jackson froze like a Republican senator at the door of a conference on global warming.

Putting a hand on his shoulder, I said, "I was surprised when Faith said she was your sister."

He turned in my direction. "Because she's white?"

"Because she has a different last name from yours."

"We have different fathers. We're half siblings." The look on Jackson's face told me neither father was much of a bargain.

I leaned on the countertop. "So she said."

"Don't listen to everything my sister says." Jackson started to leave the pantry again.

So that's who we heard Jackson arguing with on the phone in his office. "Do you and your sister talk much about her...secrets?"

Jackson took my arm and led me toward the back of the butler's pantry, a spot Noah and I had *explored* the evening before.

"We all have secrets. I keep Faith's secrets, and she keeps

mine." A large crease formed in the center of his smooth forehead. "It has been our way since we were kids."

We sat on the ledge, which thankfully Noah had cleaned last night. "It must have been tough for you as a kid."

"It would have been tougher without Faith."

"Tell me about it?"

After taking in a deep breath to turn back the pages of time, Jackson said, "Faith and I lived with our mother who, as hard and *as many times* as she tried, was unable to keep a man around the house." He added with a pained look on his face. "My mother was addicted to alcohol and drugs."

Like mother, like daughter.

"My sister and I made the beds, did the laundry, cooked the meals, and found my mother when Mom wandered in a drugged stupor to pretty much anywhere in the neighborhood. Today when kids are abused, people call Child Custody Services to have them taken into foster care. Back then, people pointed, stared, laughed, and called us names." He smiled. "Somehow Faith and I got through it…together. After my mother went to bed with her bottle du jour each night, Faith and I had this game we played in Faith's bed. Since we lived in Oklahoma, and both of us liked local history, I used our blankets and sheets to make a fort. Faith played the prairie woman, and I played the prairie man. Inside that homemade tent, our adventures knew only the limits of our imaginations. We caught our own food, fought Native Americans, raised babies, and saved the nation from Russian invaders." He laughed. "Maybe we weren't so good at history after all."

"Did you identify as a girl back then?"

He answered resentfully, "Everyone else identified *me* as a girl, except for Faith. Regardless of how I was forced to dress or behave at home, Faith knew the truth. She was the only one who saw the real *me* hiding inside, dying to get free."

"And Faith continued to be your advocate when you transitioned?"

He nodded. "When I had finished school, and saved

enough money from my previous job, I underwent the psychiatric and medical evaluations and clearances, and the hormone treatments. When it came time for the surgery, Faith gave me whatever money she had then arranged for a loan for the rest…in her name. She also stood by me during the excruciatingly painful rehab. She told me about the job here, which offered me a new start."

After scratching my head, I asked, "But why keep your transition a secret? We live in a state with civil rights protections for the transgendered. This is a college founded by two gay men, an institution with equal rights ordinances and practices to the highest order."

Looking like a prize fighter at the end of the tenth round, Jackson replied, "Laws and regulations are important for equal rights, but they don't change people's minds. Gays are the new blacks. Transsexuals are the new gays. You know how low that puts *me*?"

I exhaled in frustration.

"Think about it, Nicky. Straight people look at me and say, 'Since you are attracted to men, why didn't you just stay a woman?' Gay people see me and say, 'Since you creep out straight people, we don't want to risk losing our rights by being connected to you.' The politicians talk about their discomfort when I use a public bathroom. Hollywood makes movies where people like me are the killers. The news media says the transgendered are a threat to children. But what nobody understands is that my gender and my sexuality are about *me*, not them. After all this time, money, and torture, I'm finally the person on the outside that I've always been on the inside: the gay man that Faith knew, loved, and protected as her brother."

"I wonder if Faith is still trying to protect you."

"From whom?"

"David and Wally knew your secret, and David was blackmailing you because of it. David must have told Loptu and Millie about you. Perhaps Faith protected you to the tune of killing them all."

"My sister stopped protecting me years ago."

I hit my head in realization. "It must have just about killed you when Faith started dating David."

He laughed iniquitously. "I just about killed *her*. Nobody was happier than me when Faith dumped David."

"For his son, Kyle," I said offering a reality check.

"Kyle's a smart kid, Nicky. He's a definite step up from his father."

Sherlock was back. "Aren't you concerned that your sister is sleeping with one of her students, co-owns his porn production company, and is addicted to cocaine?" *I obviously hit a nerve.*

Jackson stood up. His long, graceful body seemed tight and rigid. "Since you asked, I am at my wit's end with Faith *and* with her destructive behavior. Her relationship with David and now David's son is *not* all right with me. Faith's advent into the porn world on the backs of our students is disgusting and disgraceful." His dark eyes lit up like charcoal ignited by a flame. "Regardless of my sister's support of me in the past, I *vow* to stop Faith if it kills me...or her!"

"You two wanna have a threesome in here?" Scotty appeared at the doorway with lust spewing from his young eyes.

Jackson pulled himself together, and responded cogently, "I was demonstrating to Nicky how to counter a stage combat attack move. We're done now. Aren't we?"

"Seems so."

After taking Jackson by the arm, Scotty said, "Then come on, you two. Our production meeting awaits."

Tyler seemed in much better spirits during the meeting as he talked passionately about the scenic design elements of the show. Ariella came to life when discussing the costumes, especially her new cape for Paul. Scotty salivated adoringly as Jackson demonstrated a new move for one of the fight scenes.

Once the faculty members left, except for Noah of course, the students arrived, appetites in tow. Ricky, Kayla, and Jan collided in the dining room, trying to be the first to present Paul Amour with his plate of goodies. Paul piously accepted all three plates, eating equally from each.

After the cast members devoured every morsel of food and drink in sight, I sent a cautionary text to Ariella about letting out the costumes. With full and expanded stomachs, the young thespians retired to the back parlor, where SuCho, the student stage manager, led a line-through of the play. I thanked the theatre gods when the students recited their lines without hesitation. I was also relieved when during the break between the acts, the cast members discussed their characters' relationships, actions, objectives, obstacles, and tactics with one another. Noah truly is a great acting teacher, not to mention a great boyfriend.

In the last few minutes of the break, the students sat in the back parlor glued to their iPhones and iPads, texting their way to carpal tunnel syndrome. Ricky, Kayla, Jan, and Paul left the other students to sit in the front parlor with their heads together: no doubt discussing their *other* performing arts outlet in Kyle's company.

After their break, SuCho screamed everyone back to attention to run their lines for Act II. During a section of the act where Paul has no lines, he wondered out to the dining room. As Noah and I finished loading the dishwasher in the kitchen, Noah shot me a Watson-like look, nodding in Paul's direction. Taking the hint, I swallowed a handful of vitamins then joined Paul at the dining room table.

Paul's skin-tight tan cashmere sweater and jeans displayed every muscle in his body, and there were plenty to display. Posing next to the cider urn like a Greek god, Paul offered a commercial smile. "Good cider, Professor."

Hearing the students doing the line-through in the distance, I said, "The show sounds great."

Paul nodded and not a strand moved on his gelled black hair. "It's a great show."

"With a great leading man."

"No arguments here." Paul toasted in my direction and

drank his cider.

"How's the porn business?"

Paul sprayed the cider onto my sweater. For the first time since I had met him four years prior as a freshman, Paul Amour looked vulnerable. "How did you find out, Professor?"

Wiping the cider off my sweater with a napkin, I said, "Let's not discuss that now." *Butch Whopper has thankfully retired.* "Let's talk about how you like working for Kyle and Professor O'Riley."

He swallowed hard. "They pay well, and on time."

"Yes, your tuition, and Ricky's tuition, and Jan's tuition, and Kayla's tuition: all paid in full."

Paul looked like a puppy that had an accident on the rug. "Are you going to tell the Dean of Students about this?"

Leaning against the table and crossing one leg over the other, I replied, "No, Paul. I'm not."

He let out a sigh of relief that could have launched a sailboat. "Thank you."

As Paul started to leave, I held on to one of his huge triceps. "Personally, I think it's a twisted business that preys on innocent young people and often gets them hooked on drugs. But I know that you aren't innocent. And I doubt you're on drugs."

He looked deep into my eyes. "I'm not stupid."

"Then why do you want to ruin your life getting involved in this business?"

He responded resolutely, "Thanks to Kyle's business, I won't have any student loans to pay off when I'm an old man in my thirties."

Thanks. "But how will you feel about *yourself*?"

Paul's V-shaped, muscular back straightened. "I know what I'm doing. Every actor starts out doing whatever films are offered to him."

"But every actor doesn't see footage of himself having sex splattered all over the internet the moment he finally becomes a star."

Paul checked himself out in the mirror over the sideboard, obviously liking what he saw. "That was way back in your day, Professor. Nowadays, a past in porn will probably help an actor's career."

I stood next to him. "For your sake, I hope you're right."

"Professor, I know what I look like. I know where my talents…lie. I'll do *whatever* it takes with *whoever* it takes to get to where I want to go in show business."

"Even working with people like Kyle and Professor O'Riley?"

"I know what you're thinking. I suspected them of committing the murders on campus too."

"Tell me about it."

Paul sat on the window seat at the bay window and used a napkin to wipe the perspiration off his forehead. I noticed a hardness in his face that wasn't there before he embarked on a career in porn. "Kyle was angry at his father for not letting him study at Treemeadow for free. Professor O'Riley wanted Professor Samson out of the picture so she could become producer. They both didn't much like the other three professors who were killed either. You probably already knew that."

I sat next to him. "Go on."

Rubbing his strong hands together, he said, "After we wrapped our first film—"

"Would that be *Muscles 101*?"

He nodded. "Ricky was already showered and gone. I was in Kyle's john getting dressed. I overheard Professor O'Riley talking to Kyle in his room. Kyle was putting away the film gear. Professor O'Riley seemed high strung and really wired."

No doubt with white powder marks under her nose.

"Kyle told Professor O'Riley that he did everything she told him to do, and now they will have plenty of money for the business."

"Did Kyle say what Professor O'Riley had told him to do?"

Paul shook his head. "At that point Kyle and Professor

O'Riley started laughing and became...*intimate* on Kyle's bed."

"You mean *intimate* like you were with Ricky, Kayla and Jan in Kyle's movies?"

Paul looked out the window at the snow-covered porch and nodded. He looked older than his years.

"When did you get out of Kyle's room?"

"After Kyle and Professor O'Riley fell asleep. I know you think that Professor O'Riley and Kyle are lowlifes. But they're honest people. And the police don't think they killed the theatre professors."

I did a double-take. "How do you know this, Paul?"

Paul looked down at his European designer shoes. "John Dickerson told me."

After a triple-take, I said, "John Dickerson? You mean, *Detective* Dickerson."

Looking around to make sure nobody was listening, Paul explained, "Since he's been on campus, John's become my...friend."

I laughed. "A *friend* who no doubt doesn't know about your porn career."

After nodding, Paul said, "John's having some problems with his wife."

"I assume exacerbated by his affair with *you*."

Paul replied unconvincingly for such a good actor, "It's not like that, Professor. John wants to make me happy. As a matter of fact, he bought the new clothes that I'm wearing tonight."

Can you say, sugar daddy?

Paul said as enthusiastic as a cheerleader dating the team quarterback, "John wants to find out who is committing the murders, so we can get back to our classes...and to the show." He smiled affectionately. "John loves the shows on campus. He's our number one fan."

Coming nose to nose with him, I asked, "And who does the good detective think committed the murders?"

Paul looked both ways then replied, "I'm not supposed to

tell anyone yet, but John and Detective Manuello, are arresting somebody for the murders tonight."

If it's Noah, I'm barring the doors and windows. "Who?"

"One of the kids from the Film Department. He's been following Jan around lately. John's afraid if they don't arrest him, he'll try to kill Jan next." Paul raised a cautioning finger. "There's my cue, Professor."

As Paul left the dining room, I looked out the window and noticed P.J. standing on my wraparound porch with a look of terror in his eyes.

CHAPTER TWELVE

After the students put on their coats, hats, scarves, and gloves and left my house to hit an ice cream shop in town, P.J. rapped on the knocker of my front door. Once his parka hung on the coat rack in the hallway, and P.J. hung on the bookcase next to it, he said in a panic, "Professor, um you have to, you know, help me!" P.J.'s straight up in the air hairstyle fit the terrified expression on his young, cherubic face.

I sat P.J. down on the sofa in the front parlor, and Noah rushed to the kitchen to make him a cup of chamomile tea.

Wringing his hands and barely holding back tears, P.J. said, "Professor, um two like detectives, you know, came to my like dorm room and stuff like that today." P.J. pulled hard on the numerous gold rings bordering his ear. "They um took my like fingerprints, a piece of my um hair, and even like cut off a thread of my coat and stuff like that. Can they um do that, Professor?"

I patted his knee in commiseration. "I'm afraid they can."

He squirmed in his seat like a fish next to a campfire. "They also like asked me why I've been, you know, poking around the um theatre building and at the like theatre at night and stuff like that."

Noah came back with the tea. Sitting on the other side of P.J., he asked, "What did you tell the detectives?"

P.J. looked at Noah then said to me, "Professor, is he your husband?"

I smiled. "No." *Not yet.*

"Do you trust him?"

I nodded. *Especially when he plays Reg, the porn promoter.*

Noah handed P.J. the tea, and said soothingly, "I'm Professor Oliver. I teach Acting in the Theatre Department at Treemeadow. Like Professor Abbondanza, I want to help you."

Satisfied that Noah was trustworthy, P.J. answered, "I um told them I'm like in love with Jan and stuff like that, but they um didn't seem to like care." P.J. looked back and forth between Noah and me like a prisoner on death row facing his lawyer and his priest. "Professors, do the um detectives like think that I, you know, had something to like do with the um murders on campus and stuff like that?"

Sounding like the father on an old situation comedy, I replied, "I'm afraid they do."

P.J.'s face turned green. "Please like don't let them, you know, arrest me and stuff like that, Professors."

As if on cue, the doorbell rang, and Noah opened the door to Detective Manuello and Detective Dickerson. P.J. with pleading eyes clung on to my arm like a life raft. I told him to stay seated on the sofa, and I met the detectives at the front door.

"What can I do for you, detectives?"

Manuello looked past me into the hallway. "We are here to arrest Peter Jacob Myers for the murders of Professors David Samson, Wally Wanker, Millie Rodriguez, Loptu Lee, and Faith O'Riley."

Dickerson added, "We received a tip that Myers is here with you."

A tip from Paul Amour no doubt.

It sunk in. After a joint double-take with Noah, I said, "Faith O'Riley has been *killed*."

Manuello nodded gravely. "Professor O'Riley was found this afternoon in her office, strangled with a rope." He gave me an icy stare. "For once your boyfriend wasn't the one who found her."

Looking somewhat relieved, Noah asked, "Who *did* find her?"

"A film student, Kyle Samson," answered Dickerson with

a glance over at my crotch.

"What evidence do you have that P.J. is the murderer, detective?" Noah asked, sounding like a television defense attorney.

Manuello rubbed one of the rolls of fat above his tight belt. "Myers' DNA is all over the crime scenes. He's been seen in the film building during the evenings, and in the theatre buildings day and night...and he isn't a Theatre major."

"That is all circumstantial evidence, detective," Noah answered dramatically, as if vying for an Emmy Award.

I moved my body to cover the view to the front parlor, and asked affectedly, "What do you believe is the student's *motivation* for the killings, detectives? *I may be competing against Noah for that Emmy Award.*

Detective Manuello rubbed his wide nose. "Your student asked Professors Samson, Rodriguez, and Lee if they would sign him into their classes when their classes were full. Each professor refused. Also, Myers is failing Professor O'Riley's Screenwriting class. The way we see it, the murders were a kind of psychotic revenge by a deranged student against all four professors for not doing what the student wanted."

"And what about Wally Wanker's murder?" I asked, instinctively opening up my body to the nonexistent audience.

Gladly joining in on the theatricality, Dickerson said as if the last line of Act I, "Since Myers is Professor Emeritus Wanker's nephew, he is the sole beneficiary in Wally Wanker's will!"

Try saying that three times fast.

P.J. ran out of the front parlor in tears. "I didn't like do it! I'm um being like framed and stuff like that! I only, you know, wanted to um get into those like theatre classes to um be near Jan and stuff like that. I am um failing like Screenwriting because I like never, you know, go to class. I barely like knew my um great uncle and stuff like that. He was my um mother's, you know, uncle. She's um back in like Texas and stuff like that. I um met him like once and um couldn't like stand the, you know, old like coot! He um called my um mother a like hillbilly and my um father a like cowpoke! He was so like old, he was like half dead and stuff like that."

During P.J.'s tirade, Detective Dickerson held P.J. while Detective Manuello handcuffed him and read him his rights.

I blocked the door to their exit, and said a la Rita Haworth, "Detectives, have pity on this boy. The only crime that P.J. Myers committed was the crime of unrequited love." *And of failing all of his classes.*

Noah took a more sensible tact. "Don't say another word until we get you a lawyer."

With tears streaming down his face, no doubt rusting his facial rings and chains, P.J. cried, "Please don't like tell my parents and stuff like that. They'll like *kill me.*"

As the detectives led P.J. out the front door, I followed them onto the wraparound porch, and called out after them, "Don't worry. We'll get you out!"

Sounding like a British television detective, Noah shouted over my shoulder, "Stiff upper lip, P.J.!"

As P.J. was seated in Detective Manuello's car, his lip ring caught on his handcuffs and P.J. screamed in pain. Noah and I stood shivering on the front porch and watched the car drive away, as P.J. shouted out the back window between sobs, "Um please like help me and stuff like that, Professors!"

We walked back inside the house and rubbed our hands together to get warm. I couldn't stand thinking of poor P.J. locked in a prison cell, no doubt on his knees before a huge, muscular, fellow convict with no remaining conjugal visits. *How come I never got arrested when I was in college!*

Noah immediately phoned an old lawyer boyfriend (*Grrrr!*) who was willing to race over to the courthouse and represent P.J. pro bono as a favor to Noah (*Grrrr!*)—and to get some guaranteed press for his new law firm.

By the time Noah and I were ready for bed, the lawyer/ex-boyfriend phoned Noah on his cell phone to report that P.J. was booked and denied bail. So I called Ariella Samson and Paul Amour and asked them to work on Detectives Manuello and Dickerson respectively.

A half hour later the lawyer/ex-boyfriend phoned again to tell Noah that bail was set, P.J. was released with a tracking device (that no doubt tangled with his body jewelry), and P.J. was instructed to not leave his lawyer's guest bedroom. P.J.'s lawyer also forbade him to talk to anyone, including the press…and us. Finally the lawyer instructed P.J. not to set foot on campus, thereby not permitting P.J. to attend his classes (not a problem).

Checking our emails in bed, Noah and I rejoiced at Martin's announcement that the Theatre Department's classes and theatrical production were back! His email also specified that Scotty Bruno will continue to teach Millie Rodriguez's classes and maintain her other duties for the remainder of the semester, and Tyler Thompson will do the same for David Samson. Martin also noted that the department office assistant, Shayla Johnson, will take over Loptu Lee's classes, Loptu's State Accreditation Faculty Committee, and her Playwriting Club. *From Shayla's notes to Martin during department meetings, I knew she liked to write, but who knew Shayla had an advanced degree?*

This led to Noah and I having a passionate, celebratory lovemaking session, which resulted in stains on the bedroom curtains. (Don't ask.) As we cuddled in bed with our bodies entwined like overactive vines, I kissed the back of his smooth neck, and asked, "Have you given up your house yet?"

Turning back to look at me, Noah asked, "What do you mean?"

"I mean the house that the college provided for you as a professor at Treemeadow. Now that you're living with me, have you told the Dean of Administration that you no longer need it?"

Noah said to his pillow, "I haven't gotten around to it yet."

I turned him around to face me. "Why not?"

"I guess I've been preoccupied with the murders…and classes starting up again." He pressed his back against my chest and wrapped my arms around him.

I nibbled his ear. "A new professor might need the house for next academic year. When are you going to tell the Dean you've moved in here with me?"

"I don't know."

Sitting up yoga style, I said, "If you're concerned you won't get tenure if people know you are gay, I think it's a little too late to worry about that."

"It's not that...."

"Then what is it?"

He sat up next to me. "I don't want to do it right now."

My stomach dropped to the first floor. "Don't you want to live here with me?"

Noah wrapped his arms around me. "I hoped and prayed for a perfect partner just like you. It took us so long to find each other, and just as long to get together."

"So the problem *is*?"

His eyes looked like pools of sapphire. "I've had relationships before this one, and I'm sure you have too."

My heart was pounding like a porn star's pelvis. "Are you saying you won't want me anymore when I get old...older?"

He squeezed my hand. "I'll always love you...and I love living in your house."

"Actually, it's the *college's* house." *There I go correcting him again. No wonder he wants to leave me.*

His handsome face sprouted worry lines. "I've been down this road before." He lowered his head. "I don't want to end up homeless if you get tired of me and you decide to move on to someone new."

After finally breathing, I laughed tenderly. "You can keep your house, as long as you live here with me forever."

Noah's gorgeous eyes welled up with tears. "What did I ever do to deserve you?"

"Hmm, let's see if we can figure that out...together."

That led to another lovemaking session that ended with stains on the rug. (Don't ask.)

* * *

The next morning, after swallowing a fistful of vitamins to reenergize from our sexual gymnastics the night before, I made a fruit and yogurt shake then sent Noah off with a white foamy kiss (Don't ask!) to teach his first class. I wasn't scheduled to teach an early morning class (Thank God, rather Martin — Is there a difference?). So I went for a work out in the campus gym.

The students who work out in the gym are generally pumped up. The faculty members who use the gym are generally not. So as I stood in my sweat clothes straining to do my third shoulders rep on the universal gym machine, I wasn't surprised to see a muscular student in my peripheral vision effortlessly doing curls with fifty pound hand weights. I was surprised, however, when the student put down the weights and moved to the foot of my machine.

"Have you heard that classes are back on, Professor? So is our show!" Paul Amour stood in the center of the gym equipment like Hercules surveying the chains that once bound him. His various muscles were on rippling display bulging out of a white tank top and black sweat shorts.

Finishing my last shoulder exercise, I took in a much-needed deep breath. Paul smelled like a combination of soap, cologne, sweat, and sperm. As my throbbing body seemed to ask me, 'Was that last rep really necessary?' I said, "Yes, Paul, I've heard the good news, but I don't have an early morning class. It seems that neither do you."

Paul leaned on my machine and his shoulders, biceps, and forearms doubled in size. "I do my work-outs in the mornings, Professor." He patted his eight-pack abs. "Gotta stay in shape for the show."

"And for your next porn film? Or has your career ended with Faith O'Riley's murder?" I asked audaciously.

Speaking softly, Paul said, "I told Kyle I'm not available until our show closes."

Moving to the next machine, I silently warned my chest of the trauma to come. "Who will produce and distribute Kyle's films with his father and Faith O'Riley both out of the picture, so to speak?"

Following me, Paul replied sotte voce, "Kyle told me he is producing and distributing the films himself."

"Really?"

He nodded. "Actually, I think Kyle prefers it that way. As Kyle said, 'It's less complications and more money' for him."

I stopped. "I thought Kyle and O'Riley were lovers."

"They were." After looking both ways to make sure no one was eavesdropping on us, Paul whispered, "Kyle told me Professor O'Riley was getting on his nerves...becoming too possessive." He smirked. "Women can be like that. They can also get too greedy. I'm bisexual, Professor. I know about these things."

A lesson from my worldly student.

"I think Kyle wants to be an independent businessman from now on."

At the chest machine, with my arms spread back like a criminal in a stockade, I pulled my arms together and groaned. "Have you told your friend, *John*, about your porn career yet?"

Paul bent down to tie his sneaker lace and his butt cheeks looked like two ripe cantaloupes on display at a farmer's market. "I'll tell John soon. I don't think he will have a problem with it."

I laughed. "Yes, our junior detective is a lover of the arts." Finishing the exercise, my arms snapped back into place like a toy skeleton and I moaned in pain.

Stretching his perfect diamond-shaped back, Paul said, "Is your student doing okay under house arrest?"

Groaning through another rep of my chest exercise, I replied, "I hope so." After an elongated groan, I added, "It wasn't very nice of you to rat P.J. out to Dickerson, but thank you for speaking to Dickerson on his behalf."

"It's the least that I can do for my director, and the keeper of my secret." Paul flexed his pecs and smiled with superiority. "Besides, I told you, John likes to do things to make me happy."

Moving back to the free weight area, and to the wall mirror, Paul energetically continued his work-out routine. I went home to take a ten-minute nap.

Upon waking in bed a half hour later with my shoulders and chest screaming at me, I showered, dressed, and drove to campus again asking myself what clue I was missing in the murders.

When I got to the theatre department building, I decided it was time for some fatherly advice (or at least a good gossip session). So I bypassed my office and stepped into the department head's outer office to see if Martin was available.

Sitting behind her desk with one ear to Martin's door, Shayla looked up, and said officiously, "He's on the phone with a textbook rep."

"That, no doubt, will take a while." I looked out the window and stared at the fluffy snow falling on the trees, benches, ponds, and lawn outside looking like sugar in a cotton candy machine. Then I picked up the snow globe on Shayla's desk and smiled at the identical winter scene.

Shayla waved to the chair next to her. "Sit. That's why we have chairs."

After complimenting Shayla on her new sweater, which showcased the same winter scene, I held up an overflowing folder on her desk, and said, "Soon you won't have to file any more forms."

Looking away from her computer screen, Shayla responded with a sarcastic laugh, "Don't I wish."

"Martin emailed us the news that you are taking Loptu's place for the rest of the semester."

She moved a strayed dark strand of hair inside the bun at her neck, and said instructively, "An office temp is taking over as department office assistant. She starts tomorrow. You know what that means?"

I shook my head like a preschooler asked if he has a favorite novelist.

Shayla poked a finger at her chest, and responded testily,

"It means that *yours truly* will be teaching Playwriting classes, going to College Accreditation Faculty Committee meetings, advising the student Playwriting Club, grading papers, updating Playwriting Curriculum and assessment reports, advising Playwriting students, *and* redoing everything the office temp does wrong in the office...meaning *everything*." Having finished her diatribe, Shayla went back to working on her computer. As her long nails clicked on the computer keyboard, Shayla said, "I'm ready for spring break, Nicky."

"Wait until you start teaching. You'll be marking the days off on your calendar."

Shayla held up her desk calendar displaying red X marks in the boxes. We shared a laugh.

Unsuccessfully trying to make eye contact with her as she worked, I said, "I never knew you had an advanced degree in Playwriting."

She patted her computer screen. "I got my MFA online. It gave me something to do during the summers when it's relatively quiet around here." She added caustically, "And summer's the only time it *is* quiet around here."

I leaned an arm on her desk. Shayla pushed it off. "Nicky, this isn't a barn back in Kansas."

Sufficiently scolded, I sat up straight, and asked, "Have you written much?" *Besides your witty gems on notes to Martin at department meetings?*

Shayla resumed typing on her computer. "I wrote some one-act plays that were done at a theatre festival in New Hampshire."

"That's great." I smiled. "You should write a play about what's been going on in our department."

Shayla opened her bottom desk drawer and held up a huge stack of papers. "Done...minus the last scene, where the murderer, rather than killing the sleuth, explains in detail why and how he killed each of the victims, mentioning all the clues the audience missed."

I nodded. "I hope you find a producer for your play."

Shayla motioned to the reporters, now sitting on the

benches outside her window. "I don't think finding a producer will be a problem. Inquiring minds and all that." She went back to her work.

Standing and pouring myself a cup of hot cocoa from a pot on a hot plate across from Shayla's desk, I said, "I also never knew you had aspirations to be a college professor."

Shayla looked over the top of her computer monitor. For the first time since I've known her, I saw a rapturous gleam in her large, dark eyes. "Being a professor is what I've wanted to do ever since I can remember, Nicky. I've always liked the college environment of faculty sharing their knowledge with students who are eager to learn."

Which college is this? "Have you tried applying for any faculty positions at other colleges?"

She laughed acrimoniously. "Dozens of them! But no department would hire a department secretary as their new Assistant Professor."

Except this one...after Loptu Lee was murdered. From the office window I could hear a local television reporter outside interviewing Detective Manuello. I said, "They should interview you, Shayla."

Shayla smiled broadly, unleashing a beautiful white smile. "You think I'm photogenic?"

"Yes. But that's not why." Leaning over her desk, I said, "You are the smartest person around here. You see everything, hear everything, and *know* everything."

"No argument there." She went back to her keyboard.

"Who do you think is our murderer?"

"It's not that kid they arrested." As she tapped away, she said, "What if it's like that Agatha Christie story, where everybody got together and decided to join forces to commit murder?"

We shared a laugh.

"I think it all has to do with sin."

I sat down and took a sip of cocoa. "How do you mean?"

"David and Wally were womanizing, back-stabbing, egomaniacal thieves. The women were their victims."

I started to rest my elbow on Shayla's desk but pulled away before she could swat at it like a fly. "I knew David had many women, but Wally seemed unlucky in love. As a matter of fact, I heard Wally tried to blackmail two female professors into having sex with him."

"That doesn't surprise me," Shayla said indignantly. "Wally did the same thing to me."

I would have fallen off the chair if it weren't for my fear that Shayla would have scolded me for scuffing the wide plank wooden floor. "When did this happen?"

"I'm older than I look." Shayla stopped typing and pointed to her middle desk drawer. "Thanks to hair dye and face creams." She took in a deep breath and continued. "Wally hired me as department secretary back when he was department head. He knew my mother was sick, and that I needed the money. When it came time for my review, Wally dangled my evaluation over me...along with his *schlong*."

"What?"

Shayla nodded then folded her hands across her chest like a child on a hunger strike. "I told Wally in no uncertain terms that I wasn't interested in playing hanky-panky with him. As pushy and obnoxious as you saw him behave as Emeritus faculty, he was even worse when he was department head." She looked down at her keyboard. "He did not take no for an answer."

"Couldn't you complain to Human Resources? File charges against Wally?"

She shook her head. "This was back in the days before sexual harassment suits were taken seriously, especially a complaint from a black woman against a white man. I knew a complaint against Wally would mean a wink and a slap on the wrist for him, and the end of employment here at the college for me."

I ran a hand through my hair, careful not to unleash any dandruff onto Shayla's desk. "So what did you do?"

"I'm not proud of this, Nicky, but I put up with Wally's good morning kisses on the cheek, his arm around my waist at the water cooler, his pinches at his desk..." She made a losing attempt at holding back tears. "...and his petting in the supply closet. I assumed it was better than losing my job...and better than giving into Wally's sexual demands."

I took her hand, and said sincerely, "I'm so sorry this happened to you."

She squeezed my hand then wiped her face with a tissue. "Thanks. I was so happy years back when Martin became department head. I cried tears of joy in his office for the first few weeks."

"I can understand why."

She threw the tissue in the waste paper basket under her desk then went back to her computer screen.

Sounding like the television newscaster outside, without the shrieking voice, I asked, "Were you ever married? Did you ever have any kids?"

"No, and no."

"How come?" I asked as if it was any of my business. "You never met the right man?"

She stopped typing and her eyes met mine. "I never met the right *woman*."

I nearly fell off my chair and out the window. "I never knew —"

"I'm a lesbian, Nicky. You can say the word."

I laughed in spite of myself. "And I guess I'm heterosexist."

"It takes years of conditioning." She winked at me. "I'm not as lucky as you and Noah. You two make a great team."

"Thanks." Unable to hold back, I kissed her on the cheek then said flippantly, "Now you can have me fired for sexual harassment."

"Who would believe *that*?"

We shared another laugh.

I said honestly, "The women in Vermont don't know what they are missing. I can't *believe* you are unattached."

Her eyes sparkled. "I was attached once. I thought she was the *one*."

Sitting at the edge of my seat and nearly falling off it again, I asked, "What was she like?"

Shayla smiled in remembrance. "She was younger than me."

Rubbing my hands together, I said, "Oooooh, you're a sugar mama."

She laughed. "She was a writer, like me. And she was wickedly funny."

"Like you."

She chuckled. "She was a good, caring person."

"Also like you." After we shared a smile, I asked, "What happened between you two?"

The lines in Shayla's face sprouted like weeds in spring. "She succumbed to a disease."

"What disease?"

She let out a long sigh. "The disease of revenge and greed." Shayla used another tissue to wipe a tear under her eye. "She did some terrible things, Nicky, and hurt a lot of people, including herself. She became a different person who I didn't know. It eventually got her killed."

"I'm sorry."

"Me, too."

I asked soberly, "When did she pass away?"

"Yesterday afternoon. Her name was Faith O'Riley. And she must have still felt something for me, because she left me half her money."

CHAPTER THIRTEEN

Later that morning, I (having not started my class yet) and Noah (having finished his class) sat in Noah's office, where I filled Noah in on my chats with Paul and Shayla.

Sitting with his feet up on his desk, Noah exercised 'the little grey cells.' "So Wally sexually harassed Shayla, Ariella, and Faith O'Riley. Shayla and Faith were lovers. Faith left half of her money to her brother Jackson and the other half to Shayla. And Shayla is our new Temporary Playwriting professor."

"Ah, life in a sleepy little New England college town," I said sitting across from him. "It seems that the Samson men were mere stepping stones on Faith's planned path to becoming a porn producer." *Try saying that three times fast.* "But Kyle ended up on top."

Noah nodded and unwrapped a packed lunch he brought for us.

As our teeth sank into our tuna salad sandwiches on eight-grain (no nut) bread, I asked, "What do you make of P.J. inheriting Wally Wanker's money?"

"P.J. had no affection for his great uncle. He got lucky, or unlucky, because Wally had no children and hated his niece, P.J.'s mother."

I downed a handful of vitamins from my pocket.

Noah pressed his knee against my thigh (which caused a hardness in my pants). "Did Shayla know if Millie's and Loptu's families are contesting their wills?"

I shook my head and nearly choked on a vitamin.

"Nicky, we need to find out!"

Coughing up the vitamin, I asked, "Why?"

"Because if Ariella and Kyle inherit from *three* wills that gives them a stronger motive than Jackson and Shayla sharing the inheritance from *one* will."

I rested my elbows on Noah's desk. "But we don't know Millie's parents or Loptu's brother, or even how to contact them."

Resting his head on my shoulder, Noah responded, "Then we need to find out."

"We can't just march into the college's Human Resources Office and ask for the contact information of Millie's and Loptu's next of kin." I remembered Mickey. "Or maybe *I* can."

He kissed my chin. "Do tell."

After kissing Noah's forehead, I said, "Before you came to Treemeadow, I dated someone in Human Resources."

Noah's eyes turned into slits. "*Dated?*"

"We went out *one* time, after which I realized he wasn't right for me."

"How come?"

"Because he wasn't *you.*"

Resting back in his chair with a self-satisfied smile, Noah said, "It's a good thing I came to Treemeadow when I did."

"No arguments here."

"What are you going to do?"

I pulled Noah off his chair and into my arms for an affectionate kiss...and butt squeeze. Feeling like Agent 00Nicky, I said, "Wait for me here, baby."

As Noah dropped into his chair, fanning himself with his napkin, I shot him a macho wink then headed across campus to Human Resources.

As is unfortunately the case at most colleges, full time faculty positions are on the decline at Treemeadow, yet administrative positions are growing like magic mushrooms at an outdoor rock concert. I walked through cubicle after cubicle of Human Resource employees, who looked like rats in a maze clicking vociferously on their computer keyboards.

With my legs throbbing from exhaustion, I finally reached the cubicle of Mickey Minor. Mickey is handsome, muscular, naturally blond, and under five feet tall. Though Mickey is close to my age, on our only date (to a movie), the box office attendant asked me if Mickey was under twelve.

"Nicky!" I heard Mickey's voice surrounded by stacks of health insurance and pension forms. Jumping out of his seat like a Munchkin greeting Glinda, Mickey wrapped his arms around my hips and pressed his face into my abdomen. "To what do I owe the pleasure of this visit?"

After returning the hug, I sat on his desk. "How are things in the land of H.R.?"

He grinned puckishly. "Still a thrill a minute." He nudged my knee. "I heard about the murders in your department. You didn't need to kill all those people to get my attention. You could have just picked up the phone and told me you missed me."

Offering my most winning smile, I said, "I'm hoping you can do me a little favor."

Mickey glanced at his watch. "I get off at five o'clock, unless you prefer a rendezvous in the break room."

I recalled why we had only one date. "Actually, I need a bit of information about two of my deceased colleagues." I added nonchalantly, "Just the contact information for their next of kin."

Sitting at his desk dejectedly, he said, "You know I can't give out personal information." He ran his tongue around his full lips. "Except about me."

I leaned in closer. "Not even for an old pal, Mickey?"

"Rules are rules."

Spreading my legs and dangling my…foot in his direction, I tried seduction. "But rules can be broken, can't they?"

Obviously melting under my powers of persuasion, Mickey hit a few keys on his keyboard, and said optimistically, "How can I service you?"

After I told him Millie's and Loptu's full names, Mickey gave me the information then sat in hopeful anticipation of *payment.* As he stood and wrapped his arms around my knees, I confided to my old friend about "the pesky herpes outbreak that had resurfaced," upon which Mickey hurried off to an urgent managers' meeting.

After class later that afternoon, I sat in Noah's office as he aimed his desk lamp in my face and interrogated me about my *past lover.* Once I filled Noah in on my escapade in H.R., I reached for my cell phone and punched in the numbers from the drool-stained note from Mickey. Loptu's brother, a Kindergarten teacher in Springfield, Ohio, answered on the fifth ring, having just gotten home from school. Affecting a Queens (meaning the place in New York) accent, I said, "Mr. Lee, this is Harvey Mishegas of Mishegas, Mishegas, and (another) Mishegas Law Firm of New York. Please accept my condolences for the loss of your sister."

Like Dr. Frankenstein admiring his monster, Noah kissed my cheek, held his hands to his heart proudly, and nuzzled his ear against the phone's earpiece.

In response to Mr. Lee's curt inquiry as to how I got his name and phone number, I replied jovially, "You should pardon my chutzpah, Mr. Lee, but I looked you up after hearing on television about the tsuris with your sister."

"The murders at Treemeadow College were reported on the television news stations in New York?" Hingsu Lee asked.

Not having Noah's background in improvisational acting, I breathed a sigh of relief when he passed me a note.

After reading Noah's missive, I said, "You know technology nowadays, Mr. Lee. My television gets two hundred bupkes news channels from all over the world. I could have plotzed when I heard on one of them about your poor sister's murder...and how she left her money to a colleague rather than to her own family." I added with an empathetic catch in my throat, "I said to myself, 'Harvey, how much would you kvetch if your shlep of a brother left his money to the schlemiels he works with at the fracking company instead of leaving it to you?' After all, blood is thicker than gas."

186

Not much friendlier than his sister's mean personality, Mr. Lee responded coldly, "I am not interested in speaking to a lawyer."

I did my best to keep him on the phone. "Feh, no problem. I don't want to give you a whole spiel, Mr. Lee. Since the beneficiary of your sister's will is also deceased, I just want to know if you plan to contest the will before *the beneficiary's* family receives payment."

Noah mimed applause in support. Unfortunately, Higsu Lee was not as taken with my performance. "Mr. Mishegas, let me save you the time and energy of continuing. My sister and I were not very close. Her personality...or personalities made that impossible. She had the right to leave her money to whomever she chose. Since she didn't choose me, I have...and want nothing to do with Loptu's baggage." He added vehemently, "So please end this *shtick* and go chase another ambulance."

Having gotten my answer from Hingsu Lee, I tried the same routine on Millie's parents in Cuba (with Noah again listening in and offering cue cards for support). Thankfully they spoke English (better than P.J. Myers), and were a great deal more accommodating than Hingsu Lee. However, the final result was the same. As Mr. Rodriguez explained before terminating my phone call, "Mr. Mishegas, my wife and I love and miss our daughter very much. Since she evidently wanted her money to go to these people, we will do our best to make sure her wish is carried out."

Staring at my cell phone, Noah said in amazement, "So Ariella and Kyle will be in for a windfall."

"It sure looks that way," I replied putting my cell phone (and the character of Mr. Mishegas) back inside my pocket.

As Noah rose to walk me to the door, he said, "We need to keep an eye on the *grieving* widow and her enterprising son."

Hooking my arm through his, I said, "Not a problem. With P.J. under his lawyer's house arrest, the police gave Martin the go-ahead for us to open the show tomorrow night!"

Noah kissed my cheek. "You'll murder them, Nicky!" He

covered his mouth. "Poor choice of words."

Wrapping my arms around Noah, I pressed his chest against mine, and said, "Ariella and Kyle will be at the opening, and so will all the other suspects."

Noah kissed me, pressed his crotch against my growing mound then whispered in my ear, "It looks like the game is *afoot.*"

After my last class I went home for a quick dinner (and a quickie with Noah) then I rushed to the theatre for our (finally) last technical dress rehearsal. Though the four leading actors looked a bit tired (I knew why!), the show went well, and we seemed ready for our first performance the following evening. Ariella was there as usual, making no mention of the wills or her son's *business venture.*

Back home that night in bed with Noah's naked body pressed against mine, and snow falling in whimsical white swirls outside our bedroom window, Noah and I looked into one another's eyes and smiled.

Noah kissed my nose. "Good luck tomorrow night."

Returning the kiss, I said, "The students are definitely ready to open." *In more ways than one.* My stomach made an audible flip flop.

Sitting up in bed, Noah said, "You can't be hungry after that dinner we ate tonight."

Noah's chicken pesto, gnocchi in cream sauce, and broccoli in gruyere cheese sauce could have fed an army after a hunger strike. I sat up, and replied, "No, dinner was delicious. As was our after-dinner *cordial.*"

Noah giggled naughtily then he took my hand, and said, "You can't be worried about the show."

I squeezed his hand. "It's not the show."

Noah leaned his back against the headboard and nodded knowingly.

"There's something about the murders that I'm missing. It's there dangling right in front of me like a carrot. Why can't I see it?"

He put his arm around me. "You'll figure it out at the right time, Nicky."

"And until I do P.J. sits under house arrest, the murderer or murderers of five of our colleagues goes unpunished, and any one of us could be next!"

Noah rested his head against mine. "I'm a little psychic sometimes, and I have the feeling there's going to be a breakthrough tomorrow night."

I pressed my knee against his, and said, "Is everyone from Wisconsin *a little psychic*?"

He smiled releasing adorable dimples. "Only the cute ones."

"Then lucky for me I got one of the cute ones."

After another lovemaking session that left stains on the fireplace mantel (Don't ask.), we fell into joint slumber.

Unfortunately, my dreams were not peaceful visions of dancing sugarplums. David's bald head sneered at me, as he said accusingly, "What's wrong with you, Nicky? The clues have been there all along, even before that knife went into my back. You never were very observant. That's one of the reasons you are not a good director. And the sole reason my murderer is still free!"

Wally Wanker's head floated by next, as he shouted, "When I was department head, *I* would have figured out who poisoned me!"

The next drifting head was Millie's. "As I was pushed off that balcony, I thought, 'Nicky will figure out who did this to me.' I guess I was wrong."

Loptu's triangular black and white hair surrounded her angry face, as she screamed, "How many more people have to be killed before you figure this out, Nicky? You are a disgrace." Then she smiled sweetly, and added, "Love to you and Noah."

Lastly Faith O'Riley's head hovered menacingly, as she said with a sniff, "Strangled with a rope? Right after I talk to Reg McCallister? Really?"

I woke with a shriek. Noah held my sweating body in his arms as my breathing and heart rate slowly left the express track.

Minutes, or maybe hours, later I fell back to sleep. This time the cast of my dreams were my living colleagues, as they maniacally cornered me in the back of the theatre. Ariella raised Paul's new cape over my head, trying to suffocate me. Jackson readied his long, flowing arms and legs in preparation of a fight move to knock me senseless. Scotty stole my college ID card, crossed off my name, and replaced it with his own. Tyler lifted a stage light over my head, and Kyle wound up to hurl a digital film camera at me. Completing the ominous circle around me, Martin and Shayla waved a schedule of classes at me, where I was scheduled to teach an 8 am class! Hovering behind a seat in the back row of the theatre, I screamed until I woke once again in Noah's doting arms. As Noah stroked my back and told me it was all a bad dream, I totally agreed.

* * *

I woke in bed surrounded by wet sheets (It's not what you're thinking). Noah and I raced through our showers and breakfast of apricot whole wheat waffles (no pine nuts for Noah) with a fruit and yogurt smoothie to chase down a ton of vitamins (for me). Before rushing out the door with my suit on a hanger, I realized that with all the commotion over the murders, I never purchased opening night gifts for my creative staff, cast, and crew. Noah came to the rescue, offering to go shopping for me then meet me at the theatre before show time with the gifts. *See why I love him so much!*

When I arrived at the theatre, I was not surprised to see my dedicated staff already engaged in last minute fixes for opening. Ariella had been in the Costume Shop all night mending torn hems and steaming creases out of pants. Dressed in black with dark circles under her eyes, she really looked like the walking dead as she ironed Paul's new cape. Tyler's long hair, gold cross on a chain, and body tattoos (lexis and graphics) swung from the top of a ladder as he replaced burnt out bulbs on stage. Jackson was in the wings running fight choreography with Paul and Ricky (to Ricky's delight), and Scotty was in the green room (backstage lounge) giving last minute notes to SuCho. The rest of the cast members were in their dressing rooms or in the theatre house going over their lines (between texting on their phones).

At lunchtime I stood center stage to make the important announcement that pizza with various toppings, courtesy of our department head, was available in the lobby. My students raced like a buffalo stampede to the theatre lobby, where they ate and texted to their hearts' delight. Ricky, Jan, and Kayla got there first to make sure Paul got three slices with his favorite topping.

While the students ate enough to feed a third world country, Ariella made a covert, whispered announcement in my ear that her homemade, giant-sized, carob raisin brownies were hidden away in the Scene Shop—for staff only. Though too nervous to eat them herself, Ariella welcomed me to enjoy. I raced to the Scene Shop, where I found Tyler, Jackson, and Scotty with carob all over their hands and faces, and two brownies remaining on Ariella's silver platter. Deliberating whether to eat one or call Noah, my appetite won out and I took a huge mouthful of the sweet, rich, delicious wonder (to see if they were nut-free). Once I finished the brownie (again just to make sure they did not have nuts), I warned Tyler, Jackson, and Scotty not to touch the last brownie, and I left a voice message on Noah's cell phone telling him to nab the amazing brownie in the Scene Shop the minute he arrives with the gifts.

For the rest of the afternoon I answered questions from cast and crew members, gave last minute directions to the crew heads, approved wardrobe and makeup, read the play program (Why is there always one typo that nobody noticed?), and gave last minute notes and well wishes to the leading actors.

When I got to my star's dressing room door, Ricky and Kayla were coming out of it.

"How come you two aren't in costume and makeup yet?" I asked in director mode.

Kayla answered with adoration in her eyes. "I was doing Paul's makeup for him."

"And I was getting Paul into his opening costume," said Ricky like a cult member at the punch table.

"I'm sure Paul appreciates the help, but don't you think it's time to get into your *own* characters?"

Kayla said like Mother Theresa, "Paul needs us, Professor."

"And we need him," Ricky added pragmatically.

I couldn't resist. "Kayla, Ricky, this may be none of my business—"

They replied in unison, "It's okay, Professor."

I put a hand on each of their shoulders. "You'll both be graduating in May. Don't you want to find someone who you don't have to…share?"

After exchanging a knowing smile with Ricky, Kayla said, "Professor, thanks for your concern, but we know what we are doing."

"Which is?" I asked in confusion.

Kayla explained, "We'd rather have a part of perfection than a whole lot of mediocrity."

Ricky added, "There are many different types of relationships and families, Professor. You should know that. We're happy with ours."

With that they went into their dressing rooms to no doubt start a Paul Amour fan club.

As I entered Paul's dressing room, Kayla and Ricky's idol was sitting at the vanity (an appropriate place for him).

"Thanks for the opening night gift, Professor."

Noah had appropriately gotten Paul a hand mirror. *Perfect gift, Noah.* "You're welcome." As I stared into his handsome face, I asked, "Why the glum look?"

Paul stared into his reflection in the mirror. "John is on duty tonight. So he can't make the opening."

I patted one of the muscles on Paul's back. "Chin up. Our

young detective will be here for one of the other performances."

Shrugging his massive shoulders, Paul looked up at me, and said, "But there is only one opening night."

I smiled. "And it is *your* night, Paul. You worked long and hard for it. Enjoy it."

Returning the smile, Paul said, "I will, Professor." Then he winked. "And the audience will enjoy it even more."

And he's back.

As I started to leave, Paul said, "Professor, there's something you should know."

Were you nominated for a GayVN Award?

"Ricky, Jan, Kayla, and I are giving up our...*other* career."

I smiled. "I'm glad to hear that, Paul. What changed your minds?"

Adding a bit more rouge to his already rosy cheeks, Paul responded, "I thought about what you said...about my future. And I want to do projects that I, and my kids, will be proud of, Professor. And I want the same thing for my friends."

Thinking of Detective Dickerson, I said, "I have the feeling I'm not the only one responsible for your new revelation."

Paul's chiseled features softened as he looked up at me. "I guess that's one of the perks of hanging around people so much older than me."

I left his dressing room while I was still young enough to walk. "Have a good show."

Upon entering Jan's dressing room across the hall, I marveled at my show's beautiful leading lady. Dressed in a floor length yellow gown with her blonde hair laced with yellow ribbons, Jan stood fastening a stunning gold necklace.

"The necklace is perfect for your character."

Jan giggled. "Totally, Professor."

I moved closer to examine it more carefully. "It's not from the prop closet, is it?"

She shook her head causing the ribbons in her hair to dance merrily. "It was like a gift...from um P.J. Myers from your, you know, Directing class."

Smiling, I replied, "P.J. has good taste."

Jan sat in front of the wall mirror combing her hair. "He like bought me lots of totally cool, you know, gifts all semester."

Sounding like my department head, I said, "P.J. likes you. What do you think about him?"

While freshening her lipstick, Jan said, "He's um a nice guy, Professor."

"But he's no Paul Amour?"

Jan turned to face me. I noticed tears brimming in her lined eyes. "Professor, I um know that you are like aware of our...*stint* in the Film Department. Kayla, Ricky, and I um only did that to be like near Paul." She looked down in embarrassment. "And now Paul is, you know, with Detective Dickerson."

Bending on one knee (I can still do that, Paul) next to her, and lifting her chin to meet mine, I said convivially, "Jan, you may not believe this but I was young once too, and, like you, I made a lot of mistakes, including falling for the wrong guy—more than once." I took her powdered hand. "Making mistakes is part of growing up. But not learning from them...isn't."

She nodded and wiped her eyes with a tissue, careful not to dislodge her fake eyelashes.

Noticing a gift envelope with her name on it resting on the vanity, I asked, "Did you like your opening night gift?"

"Professor, did you um get me a like phone calling card because I text in class so much?"

Very clever, Noah! "Actually, I'm hoping you will use it to phone someone who doesn't have a lot of friends right now."

"Um who, Professor?"

I looked at her necklace, and responded, "Someone who would like very much to hear from you." I smiled. "Have a good show."

After I left Jan's dressing room, the rest of the cast and crew thanked me, seemingly delighted with their opening night gifts.

Next, I checked in with the box office staff. To my delight we were sold out for the entire run of the show. *Amazing what five murders can do to a show's ticket sales.*

Then I went to my office in the next building for a quick take-out dinner and lots of vitamins for energy. Finally, I changed into my gray suit and headed back to the theatre lobby to welcome the audience members.

First to arrive, of course, was Noah, looking gorgeous in a dark blue suit with a red tie. His curly blond hair, cascading over his neck, made me summon up every ounce of willpower I had not to throw him into the box office booth and ravage him. After filling me in on his day (purchasing, wrapping, and delivering my opening night gifts to the cast and crew—after stopping off at the Scene Shop as I had asked), Noah smiled at me lovingly, and said, "Good luck tonight, Nicky." Then he growled softly in my ear. "You look amazing."

Growling louder, I replied, "You look more amazing."

We kissed and heard a "Tsk" sound coming from nearby. I looked over at an elderly man with his arm around an elderly woman. (The audience members over eighty years old are always the first to arrive.) The blue-haired woman, wearing sequenced sweat clothes, sneered like a debutante in a flooded sewer in the Middle East.

I asked politely, "May I help you with something, madam?"

"Young man," the woman said haughtily, "I understand that you people have the right to *so-called* marriage now, but can you explain to me why you people must constantly flaunt it out in public in the faces of *innocent* people?"

"I will be happy to, madam." I responded like a pre-school teacher teaching the primary color chart, "Since the divorce rate of opposite-sex couples is double the divorce rate of same sex couples, we are trying to teach you how to do it *right*."

The woman glared at her husband in a rage. "Walter, are you going to let this *deviant* talk to me like that?"

195

"It's about time *somebody* did, Estelle." The gentlemen removed his arm from around his wife's shoulders and walked off toward the restrooms (probably for the third time that hour).

His wife chased after him screaming, "What did you mean by that? I asked you, what did you mean by that? Is your hearing aid on? Walter, did you hear me? Are you listening to me, Walter?"

After we shared a laugh, Noah said, "I guess that makes one more divorce for their side."

Since it was a half hour before show time, patrons of all ages, shapes and sizes flooded the theatre lobby. Among them were Ariella and her son Kyle (both in black), Shayla our department office assistant (decked out in a gold lamé dress and matching purse), Scotty and Jackson (donning their gay apparel in a yellow and red suit respectively), Tyler with his hair tied back for the occasion (having turned in his overalls for a blue polo shirt and slacks), and Martin (wearing a silver bowtie and sweater vest) and his spouse Ruben (dressed in a silver suit). As I watched my department head and his husband whisper and giggle merrily together, I hoped that Noah and I would one day reach the pinnacle of forty years together.

As student ushers opened the theatre doors, audience members waved their tickets to gain entrance into the theatre. As my colleagues passed by, they cordially wished me good luck. In each case I responded with a very self-assured, "thank you," as my heart raced and my stomach churned in anticipation of the start of the premiere performance.

I took my seat in the theatre next to Noah and offered up a prayer for theatre magic. The house lights dimmed, and the stage lights came up. At some point I started breathing. The first act went very well. The energy on stage and in the audience was high. The set, props, costumes, projections, and film clips perfectly highlighted the mood of the show. The leading actors were in top form giving their best performances yet. Paul's handsome, virile, menacing stage persona caused many women, and men, in the audience to audibly swoon to near orgasm (as it did Ricky, Jan and Kayla on stage).

At intermission in the lobby, I received numerous accolades and pats on the back. After giving me a joint thumbs-up, Scotty and Jackson sat with their heads (and lips) together on the red velvet bench in the turreted area of the lobby, causing another rousing argument between Estelle and Walter.

After raving to me about the various merits of the play, particularly the, "brilliant directing," Martin and Ruben sat in the lobby window seat reviewing and commenting on the play program.

Ariella squeezed my shoulder and told me the play was, "pure magic, especially the costumes."

Tyler gave me a high-five and his Nahum 1:2 tattoo nearly grazed my face. "Thanks for the cool collaboration on an amazing show."

Shayla pinched my bottom, and said with a gleam in her dark eyes, "If you go to Broadway and don't take me with you, you'll be victim number six."

Lastly, Noah threw his arms around me, and said adoringly, "I am so proud of you...and so proud to be *with* you."

After we shared a hug, the lobby lights flickered, and we took our seats for Act II.

I sat back in my seat and enjoyed Act II. The energy was even higher than in Act I. The actors were even more believable and charismatic, and they worked together more smoothly as an ensemble. The more difficult technical effects went off without a hitch. The audience laughed, wept, and gasped in all the right places.

As the play drew to a close, the dead bodies on stage (Ricky's being the last) artfully dripped blood in front of a flashing and rotating red cyclorama. Paul strutted through the street set of Victorian lampposts and building facades with his long, flowing red cape weaving from dead body to dead body. Finally, Paul held up the bloody knife (fake this time), and delivered his last line as if in multiple orgasm with the audience, "The Lord is vengeful and strong in wrath. And revenge is oh so sweet!"

The lights faded to black. The audience exploded in applause that grew in intensity during the curtain call and erupted like a volcano at Paul's final bow.

As the stage lights blackened and the house lights came up, I jumped out of my seat, and shouted, "I know who did it."

Rising from his seat next to mine, Noah said smiling, "We all do *now*. Bravo! What a terrific show."

I clutched at Noah's suit lapels fervently. "No, I know who killed our colleagues." Whipping my cell phone out of my suit pocket, I frantically began punching numbers.

"Who are you calling?" Noah asked while casing the theatre house.

"Detective Manuello. I have to tell him."

Noah took the cell phone from my hands. "Don't do it."

"But I know who killed —"

"Don't do it *here*...in *public*." Noah looked around the auditorium at the students, faculty, staff, parents, and community patrons. "The murderer could hear his or her name and come after *you*." He held my hand. "It took me this long to find you, Nicky. I won't lose you now." He put my phone in his pocket. "Make the call in your office. Tell Manuello who you think did it. I'll stay here and tell everyone you'll be back soon."

After a quick kiss from Noah, I raced from the theatre amidst shouts of congratulations and hands slapping my back. Not bothering to get my coat in the Scene Shop, I rushed into the theatre building next door and practically flew into my office. Before I finished pressing the numbers on my office phone to call Manuello, Martin entered my office and closed the door behind him.

"Put the phone down, Nicky," said Martin with a peculiar look in his eyes.

Chapter Fourteen

My department head looked at me apprehensively. "I overheard what you said to Noah in the theatre."

"Then you know why I have to call Detective Manuello right away." I continued punching numbers into the phone.

He took the phone from me and hung it up. "*Please*, think about what you are doing."

"I *have* thought about it, and I finally figured out the identity of murderer. It was there all the time right in front of me, Martin, but I was too preoccupied to see it." I reached for the phone again.

He grabbed my arm. "Listen to me. If you tell Detective Manuello your theory, and you are wrong, you could make a strong enemy of one of your colleagues, and cause embarrassment to the depart—"

"It all makes sense now. Every piece of this insane puzzle has finally come together in my head. The murderer is—"

He covered his ears. "Don't tell me!"

"You actually don't want to know something about the department?"

After resting a hand on my shoulder, Martin said, "You know I will support you and Noah in anything. But I don't want to be a party to having one of my colleagues arrested for murder on a whim."

"Even if one of your colleagues is a *murderer*?"

"I don't want to see you and Noah hurt."

"You were the one who asked us to investigate. I have to do this!"

Martin walked to the door. "Do what you have to do. But

be safe."

After Martin left, I pressed the buttons on my office phone rapidly.

Ariella opened the office door. "I've been looking everywhere. I'm glad I found you."

Getting Manuello's voice mail, I hung up the phone, and asked Ariella, "Where's Manuello?"

She raised her dark eyes to her black bangs. "There was some trouble downtown with a bunch of teenagers at the mall. Jose…Detective Manuello is coming here when he's finished."

"Ariella, the minute Manuello gets here, tell him that I need to talk to him. Will you do that for me? Please?"

After patting my arm, Ariella said, "No worries."

I sucked in as much air as I could get inside my lungs. "Thanks."

Ariella smiled. "Great show, Nicky. Were you happy with the costumes?"

"They were perfect," I said as I checked my watch.

At my office doorway, she added, "My brownies were a hit, too. Every one of them is gone."

Alone again in my office, I remembered Paul's comment that Detective Dickerson was on duty nearby. As I lifted the phone to call Dickerson, I heard the door open, and Tyler walked in—pointing a gun at my face.

"Put down the phone, Nicky, and sit down."

With my heart pounding in my ears, I hung up the phone and sat in my desk chair. Tyler took the seat next to me, continuing to aim the gun at my forehead.

"I heard what you said in the theatre. What gave me away?" Tyler asked with a creepier than usual look on his unshaven face.

I'll take, 'Stalling for Time Until Ariella Gets Back with Manuello' for…my life. "You really want to know?"

Tyler waved the gun near my nose. "I must."

I nodded obediently. "When you raised your arms to give me a high-five before the show started, I read your tattoo:

'Nahum 1:2.' That's the line from the Bible that Paul's character quotes at the end of the show."

He recited it like a sacred pledge of honor. "'The Lord is vengeful and strong in wrath.' I showed that five times so far. Well, actually six. And people say there's no proof that God exists." He continued, looking pleased with himself. "That's how I got this gun. Detective Dickerson was at the stage door with flowers for Paul after the show. I took the flowers and promised to deliver them to Paul, which I did. But first I hit Dickerson over the head with a Fresnel and took his gun. The Lord will help me take care of Paul, Ricky, Jan, and Kayla after the play closes." He poked me in the shoulder with the barrel of the gun. "We don't want anything to ruin our great show, do we? There's plenty of time for me to eighty-six the young porn stars."

I calculated how quickly it would take me to reach my office phone.

Tyler noticed. "There's no point trying to call anyone, Nicky." He looked at his watch. "It's been about nine hours since you ate that brownie. Rat poison takes five to twelve hours to cause enough internal bleeding to kill human beings. So you should be begging and pleading in vain at your judgment any time now."

"You poisoned Ariella's brownies after she left them in the Scene Shop?"

Tyler raised his hand. "I cannot tell a lie." He smiled proudly. "One giant-sized brownie for Scotty, one for Jackson, one for Noah, and one for you. Leviticus 18:22. Check." He made an invisible check mark in the air with his index finger.

Noah! I called Noah and told him to eat a brownie! "Tyler, how can you be so vicious?"

"I'm not vicious. As I said at your house before the production meeting, I'm really saddened and fearful for each one of you. Just imagine how awful it will be for you to face every sin you've committed while burning in the fires of Hell."

I glared at him in a rage. "What about the sins that *you've* committed, Tyler...including *murder*?"

Tyler looked offended. "It wasn't *me* who punished those people, Nicky. It was *the Lord*. I am simply *His* instrument, Nicky." He added pompously, "After Martin gives me David's position, our oh-so gay department head will be next. Then Martin can wave his colored napkins in Hell!"

Rising in anger, I said, "Whatever happened to not judging others?"

Using the gun to wave me back into my seat, Tyler responded cockily, "I am a soldier of God. *His* word in the Bible says that what you are is a sin." He waved the cross dangling from his neck. "I didn't write the book, Nicky. I just follow it."

Sitting back in my chair, I said, "Many of the books in the Bible were written in the First Century. Do you also advocate slavery, and stoning people to death for eating shellfish and wearing clothing made of more than one fabric?"

Tyler answered like the teacher's pet at a Young Nazis' convention. "It's all in the story of Sodom."

"Which is about lust, greed, and hate." I added as if facing a glowing pile of straw at the Salem Witch trials, "You ought to know about *hate*!"

Leaping behind me, Tyler wrapped his arm under my neck, yanked me from my office chair, and held the gun to my temple. "I told you that I don't hate anybody, Nicky! *You* are the one discriminating against *me* and *my* religious beliefs by telling *me* that *I* can't follow God's word. *You* are persecuting *me*!"

"By trying to stop you from murdering all of us?"

After pushing me back into my chair, Tyler said maniacally, "Thanks to the brownies, *His* will shall be done."

As I looked around the room for a possible weapon, I asked, "Is that what you teach the students in the Christian Fellowship Club?"

Tyler sighed in disgust. "Those kids are delusional." He added in a mock falsetto voice, "Red letter *liberal* Christians."

He groaned. "They only believe what Jesus is quoted to say in the Bible, written in red. How ridiculous is that?"

"As I remember from Sunday school back in Kansas, the sermons and parables, written centuries after Jesus' death by the way, are about love and serving others."

He shouted angrily, "But the rest of the Bible gives the *full* picture of God's anger and retribution against those who sin against Him: floods, locusts, hurricanes, wars, and death to the unbelievers and unrighteous!"

Why don't I feel nauseous, weak, or in pain? I ate my brownie before Noah must have eaten his. "Then why doesn't God tell us that?"

Tyler's face grew cold and threatening. "God doesn't need to prove himself."

I have to keep Tyler talking until Manuello finds me, to save Noah, and to save myself. "But you would. To Him. Why did you kill the others?"

Tyler sat back down in his chair. Using the muzzle of the gun to count on his fingers, he said arrogantly, "Let's see, after our first tech dress rehearsal for the show, I dodged Scotty, so he had to bring the real knife to David for polishing, thereby setting up anyone who talked to David in his office that night as David's possible murderer. But *I* stabbed David in his office since he had committed the sins of stealing, blackmailing, and adultery. God's will be done." Tyler moved on to his next finger. "I used rat poison from the Scene Shop to poison Wally's morning coffee in the department conference room, since Wally committed the sins of stealing and blackmailing." The gun grazed Tyler's third finger. "After you and Noah left Millie's house, I visited her pretending to have a message from David and pushed her off her balcony for committing the sins of having sex out of wedlock and getting an abortion." Readying his last two fingers, Tyler said haughtily, "I put rat poison in Loptu's tea as retribution for her part in David's adultery, and I strangled Faith O'Riley with some discarded rope from the Scene Shop since she had sex out of wedlock and produced pornography." He added in irritation, "David's creepy kid, Kyle, had just left her, so God told me to save knocking off the big porn director for another day."

Where the hell is Manuello? "Though I don't read Hebrew or Greek, I don't remember reading about abortion, producing pornography, or same-sex marriage in the Bible."

Obviously agitated, Tyler rose and came face to face with me. "I know what you are doing. You're trying to stall until that moron detective finds us." Tyler went to the window and looked outside. "No such luck, Nicky. Any minute now, you and your sodomite lover will be Satan's toast due to your *unnatural* behavior."

I'd had enough of Tyler's obvious insanity. "And waving around a gun is *natural*?"

"It was Adam and Eve, Nicky, not Adam and *Steve*!"

"Well now it's Nicky and Noah." With Tyler looking out the window, I seized my opportunity and dove on top of him, sending the gun flying to the other side of the office. Tyler and I rolled on the floor, each of us landing a punch with each spin. Though short, the many hours Tyler worked in the Scene Shop paid off for him. My hours in the gym, and my quest to protect Noah, paid off more. Kneeling next to him, I had Tyler in a headlock and was about to deliver the final blow, when Tyler elbowed me in the groin (an obviously large target). I fell backward with a yelp.

Tyler straddled my hips and used one of his hands to grasp my wrists to the floor behind me, and the other hand to squeeze my throat closed. His hands were thick, rough, and strong. As I tried unsuccessfully to loosen his grasp, I saw my life pass before my eyes. When Noah entered my replayed life, my gorgeous partner walked through my office door.

Not sure if I was dreaming or awake, I watched Noah bend down, pick up the gun, and point it at Tyler. "Get off my boyfriend or, as in biblical days, I will make you a *eunuch*!"

I blacked out.

* * *

A white light shone from the distance. Should I walk toward the light to receive my reward? What if it's not a reward? Maybe I should just stay put for a bit.

"Nicky, Nicky wake up."

Noah? Is that you? Are we in brownie gay heaven together?

I opened my eyes and squinted at the ceiling light over me. I felt a squeeze on my hand and turned my head to see Noah's beautiful face. *I am definitely in heaven.*

I squeezed his hand back, and said hoarsely, "I think this is when I'm supposed to say, 'I love you,'"

Tears flowed down his smooth cheeks. "I love you too."

After an unsuccessful attempt at sitting up, I rested my head on the pillow. "Where am I?"

Not letting go of my hand, Noah answered gently, "You're in the hospital. We've been here since last night. You've got some bruises and a light concussion, but the doctor on duty said you'll be fine."

Everything came back to me like a movie playing in my head on fast forward. "Thank you for coming after me last night, Noah."

He smiled tenderly. "Always, Nicky."

"Are you okay?"

"I'm fine." He kissed my cheek.

"But I told you to eat one of Ariella's brownies. Tyler poisoned them."

Noah shook his head and his gorgeous blond curls bounced freely. "When I got to the theatre I asked Ariella if they had nuts in them."

"There weren't any nuts in them, Noah. That's why I told you to eat one."

"Ariella explained that she used almond *extract*, so I didn't take one."

"Good move not listening to me." I kissed his hand and my throat ached from the tussle with Tyler. "But *I* ate a brownie. How come it didn't kill me?"

Noah fluffed my pillow and smiled dotingly. "The doctor

said the vitamin K you take every day blocks the effects of warfarin and coumatetralyl."

"I knew those vitamins would save me one day."

"And they did, Nicky!"

I remembered my colleagues who also ate the brownies. "What about Scotty and Jackson?"

"We're over here!"

Noah parted the white curtain next to my bed, revealing Scotty and Jackson lying in the beds nearby, attached to a vitamin K drip.

"It's about time you asked about us, Nicky," Jackson said with mock disapproval.

"How *are* you two?" I asked straining my neck to see them.

"Having your stomach pumped isn't as bad as it sounds. The technician was built like Atlas. I'd have let him stick a hose *anywhere* inside me."

Jackson hit Scotty playfully. Then they looked at one another amorously and held hands.

I whispered in Noah's ear, "Are Jackson and Scotty an item now?"

"Seems so," Noah whispered back. "They had a long talk this morning, which I *accidentally* overheard. They shared one another's pasts and vowed to share their presents...and futures."

Remembering Tyler's latest escapade, I asked Noah, "How is Detective Dickerson?"

Noah motioned to the right. "He's in the next room. The doctor said he has a concussion but he will be fine. Paul hasn't left his bedside since last night."

Last and definitely least, I asked, "Where's Tyler?"

As if on cue, Detective Manuello entered, followed by Ariella. Manuello nodded to each of us then said with a contented grin on his face, "I am sure you will all be happy to know that Mr. Thompson is being held in prison on five counts of murder and four counts of attempted murder. I don't think he is going anywhere for a *very* long time."

Ariella added with a flip of her long, dark hair and a

twinkle in her dark eyes, "Which is no doubt good news to Tyler's gigantic Muslim cell mate."

"Really?" responded Scotty. "Maybe *I* should commit a crime."

Jackson said, "Detective, the nurse should be bringing lunch soon. Is there any of that rat poison left?"

After Jackson and Scotty shared an adoring laugh, Detective Manuello scratched each of his stomach rolls, and said officiously, "Professor Abbondanza, you will also be happy to know that P.J. Myers has been released from his lawyer's house arrest."

Hopefully he will go to his classes, and we'll all be back soon to teach ours!

"There's just one loose thread that we haven't been able to solve." Manuello and Ariella sat on the two chairs facing my bed, and Manuello continued. "During the investigation, we received a number of tips asking us to talk to an actor named Butch Whopper and a writer by the name of Reggie McCallister." He rubbed his wide nose. "Funny, we haven't been able to find them."

Noah said, "They are probably right under your nose, detective."

"That's what I'm thinking," responded Manuello with a smile.

Scotty and Jackson shared a quick kiss. Detective Manuello and Ariella followed their lead, leaving Noah and me the only two people in the room not kissing.

Feeling the pain in my cheeks, I asked, "Noah, can you hold up that hand mirror, so I can see my face?"

"You sure you want me to do that, Nicky?"

I nodded. Noah took the hand mirror from the night table and placed it in front of my face.

Examining my black and blue cheeks and neck, I said, "I've looked worse when I didn't sleep and take my vitamins."

"Thank goodness you took them yesterday."

"Amen."

Noah and I shared a gentle but very romantic kiss.

EPILOGUE

The show had a successful run leading to a welcomed spring break and eventual May graduation (including for P.J. Myers who had used his time under house arrest to catch up on his assignments). After my summer vacation (at a tropical resort with Noah), the first day of fall semester arrived faster than a sore tooth at 5:01 pm on a Friday.

As Noah and I ate our breakfast in the kitchen nook (tofu scrambled eggs with spinach— and almond milk chasing down a stack of vitamins for me), I thought about our recently-graduated students. Paul Amour had already landed a leading role in a network television series. Enjoying the actor's life, Paul flew to Los Angeles over the summer with his manager (a recently divorced John Dickerson) and Paul's entourage (Ricky and Kayla). Since Paul will be playing a young detective on the television series, Dickerson will no doubt give his partner some *first-hand personal* advice while Ricky and Kayla head Paul's fan club.

P.J. (having let his piercings close while under house arrest) and Jan (conveniently forgetting her past in porn) had used Jan's jewelry, wigs, and false eyelashes from the play to become a televangelist couple with a successful fundraising show on a tax-exempt religious cable television channel. There was rumor that P.J. was being groomed by the Republican Party to run for political office.

Kyle Samson was tapped to head the New Projects Division of a film, television, and Broadway production company specializing in entertainment for family audiences. His mother, Professor Ariella Manuello, and his stepfather,

Detective Jose Manuello, could not be more proud of him. Ariella's only wish is that Kyle's father, David, was still alive to witness his son's success.

As Noah and I stood in front of the office assistant's desk in our department head's office, Shayla winked at us. "Welcome back, you two lovebirds."

Noah and I each kissed one of her cheeks, and said in unison, "Congratulations on your play getting produced."

Dressed in a blouse and skirt of deep orange, red, and yellow, Shayla perfectly matched the leaves that swayed magnificently from the trees outside her office window. Shayla swept a loose hair back into the bun at her neck and waved her hand at us dismissively. "It's just a local production by a semi-professional theatre company. It isn't Broadway." She winked at us.

Always thinking about others, Noah asked, "Will you miss teaching Playwriting?"

She patted her desk. "I prefer staying right here."

"Because of your devotion to the faculty?" I asked.

Shayla grinned. "No, because the students drove me crazy."

"And I need Shayla right where she is," Martin explained before turning to us. "How are my favorite colleagues? Come in you two."

Once seated in our department head's office on tall, leather wingback chairs in front of the cherry wood fireplace mantel surrounding a roaring fire, Noah and I smiled at one another. It felt good to be back.

Martin, wearing an orange bowtie and sweater vest, passed out monogrammed orange cloth napkins and delicate china cups filled to the brim with steaming hot cocoa, which Noah and I drank heartily.

"Congratulations on getting tenure, Noah," said our department head proudly as he sat across from us.

Noah smiled. "Thank you, Martin. Your support means more to me than you know." He pinched my knee. "As does Nicky's."

Martin waved his small hand at Noah like a cat swatting at a fly. "Your hard work and dedication to our students and our department got you tenure, Noah."

"Here! Here!" I toasted to Noah.

Noah's milky cheeks turned adoringly rosy-red.

Drinking his cocoa then wiping his mouth with his napkin, Martin said warmly, "And thank you for giving up your house, Noah. With all the new faculty members we've hired in the department over the summer, we can certainly use it."

Noah took my hand. "It was time."

For once I didn't correct him.

"Scotty moving in with Jackson has also been of great help," said Martin happily. "I think he will make a very good professor of Technical Theatre."

"As do I," I said meaning it.

"Last term was quite a semester," Martin said.

"While I'm happy things calmed down, I have to admit I miss the thrill of the chase," I said.

"Maybe someday you boys will perform an encore." Walking us to the door, Martin added, "In the meantime, I wish both of you gentlemen a wonderful semester." His eyes twinkled, "And make sure you tell me *all* the details."

As we passed Shayla's desk, she echoed her boss. "I want to get it all down for my new play."

Once outside, Noah and I stood under a multicolored maple tree next to the bronze monuments of the two founders of Treemeadow College, and we shared a long, passionate kiss.

About the Author

Bestselling author **Joe Cosentino** was voted Favorite LGBT Mystery, Humorous, and Contemporary Author of the Year by the readers of Divine Magazine for *Drama Queen*. He also wrote the other novels in the Nicky and Noah mystery series: *Drama Muscle, Drama Cruise, Drama Luau, Drama Detective, Drama Fraternity, Drama Castle, Drama Dance*; the Dreamspinner Press novellas: *In My Heart/An Infatuation & A Shooting Star*, the Bobby and Paolo Holiday Stories: *A Home for the Holidays/The Perfect Gift/The First Noel, The Naked Prince and Other Tales from Fairyland*; the Cozzi Cove series: *Cozzi Cove: Bouncing Back, Cozzi Cove: Moving Forward, Cozzi Cove: Stepping Out, Cozzi Cove: New Beginnings, Cozzi Cove: Happy Endings* (NineStar Press); and the Jana Lane mysteries: *Paper Doll, Porcelain Doll, Satin Doll, China Doll, Rag Doll* (The Wild Rose Press). He has appeared in principal acting roles in film, television, and theatre, opposite stars such as Bruce Willis, Rosie O'Donnell, Nathan Lane, Holland Taylor, and Jason Robards. Joe is currently Chair of the Department/Professor at a college in upstate New York and is happily married. Joe was voted 2nd Place Favorite LGBT Author of the Year in Divine Magazine's Readers' Choice Awards, and his books have received numerous Favorite Book of the Month Awards and Rainbow Award Honorable Mentions.

Connect with this author on social media

Web site: http://www.JoeCosentino.weebly.com
Facebook: http://www.facebook.com/JoeCosentinoauthor
Twitter: https://twitter.com/JoeCosen
Amazon: http://Author.to/JoeCosentino
Goodreads: https://www.goodreads.com/author/show/4071647.Joe_Cosentino

And don't miss any of the Nicky and Noah mysteries by Joe Cosentino

DRAMA QUEEN

It could be curtains for college theatre professor Nicky Abbondanza. With dead bodies popping up all over campus, Nicky must use his drama skills to figure out who is playing the role of murderer before it is lights out for Nicky and his colleagues. Complicating matters is Nicky's huge crush on Noah Oliver, a gorgeous assistant professor in his department, who may or may not be involved with Nicky's cocky graduate assistant and is also the top suspect for the murders! You will be applauding and shouting Bravo for Joe Cosentino's fast-paced, side-splittingly funny, edge-of-your-seat, delightfully entertaining novel. Curtain up!

Winner of *Divine Magazine*'s Readers' Poll Awards as Favorite LGBT Mystery, Crime, Humorous, and Contemporary novel of 2015!

DRAMA MUSCLE

It could be lights out for college theatre professor Nicky Abbondanza. With dead bodybuilders popping up on campus, Nicky, and his favorite colleague/life partner Noah Oliver, must use their drama skills to figure out who is taking down pumped up musclemen in the Physical Education building before it is curtain down for Nicky and Noah. Complicating matters is a visit from Noah's parents from Wisconsin, and Nicky's suspicion that Noah may be hiding more than a cut, smooth body. You will be applauding and shouting Bravo for Joe Cosentino's fast-paced, side-splittingly funny, edge-of-your-seat entertaining second novel in this delightful series. Curtain up and weights up!

2015-2016 Rainbow Award Honorable Mention

DRAMA CRUISE

Theatre professors and couple, Nicky Abbondanza and Noah Oliver, are going overboard as usual, but this time on an Alaskan cruise, where dead college theatre professors are popping up everywhere from the swimming pool to the captain's table. Further complicating matters are Nicky's and Noah's parents as surprise cruise passengers, and Nicky's assignment to direct a murder mystery dinner theatre show onboard ship. Nicky and Noah will need to use their drama skills to figure out who is bringing the curtain down on vacationing theatre professors before it is lights out for the handsome couple. You will be applauding and shouting Bravo for Joe Cosentino's fast-paced, side-splittingly funny, edge-of-your-seat entertaining third novel in this delightful series. Curtain up and ship ahoy!

DRAMA DETECTIVE

Theatre professor Nicky Abbondanza is directing *Sherlock Holmes, the Musical* in a professional summer stock production at Treemeadow College, co-starring his husband and theatre professor colleague, Noah Oliver, as Dr. John Watson. When cast members begin toppling over like hammy actors at a curtain call, Nicky dons Holmes' persona onstage and off. Once again Nicky and Noah will need to use their drama skills to figure out who is lowering the street lamps on the actors before the handsome couple get half-baked on Baker Street. You will be applauding and shouting Bravo for Joe Cosentino's fast-paced, side-splittingly funny, edge-of-your-seat entertaining fifth novel in this delightful series. Curtain up, the game is afoot!

Coming soon:

DRAMA FRATERNITY

Theatre professor Nicky Abbondanza is directing *Tight End Scream Queen*, a slasher movie filmed at Treemeadow College's football fraternity house, co-starring his husband and theatre professor colleague, Noah Oliver. When young hunky cast members begin fading out with their scenes, Nicky and Noah will once again need to use their drama skills to figure out who is sending the quarterback, jammer, wide receiver, and more to the cutting room floor before Nicky and Noah hit the final reel. You will be applauding and shouting Bravo for Joe Cosentino's fast-paced, side-splittingly funny, edge-of-your-seat entertaining sixth novel in this delightful series. Lights, camera, action, frat house murders!

DRAMA CASTLE

Theatre professor Nicky Abbondanza is directing a historical film at a castle in Scotland, co-starring his spouse, theatre professor Noah Oliver, and their son Taavi. When historical accuracy disappears along with hunky men in kilts, Nicky and Noah will once again need to use their drama skills to figure out who is pitching residents of Conall Castle off the drawbridge and into the moat, before Nicky and Noah land in the dungeon. You will be applauding and shouting Bravo for Joe Cosentino's fast-paced, side-splittingly funny, edge-of-your-seat entertaining seventh novel in this delightful series. Take your seats. The curtain is going up on steep cliffs, ancient turrets, stormy seas, misty moors, malfunctioning kilts, and murder!

Drama Dance

Theatre professor Nicky Abbondanza is back at Treemeadow College directing their Nutcracker Ballet co-starring his spouse, theatre professor Noah Oliver, their son Taavi, and their best friend and department head, Martin Anderson. With muscular dance students and faculty in the cast, the Christmas tree on stage isn't the only thing rising. When cast members drop faster than their loaded dance belts, Nicky and Noah will once again need to use their drama skills to figure out who is cracking the Nutcracker's nuts, trapping the Mouse King, and being cavalier with the Cavalier, before Nicky and Noah end up stuck in the Land of the Sweets. You will be applauding and shouting Bravo for Joe Cosentino's fast-paced, side-splittingly funny, edge-of-your-seat entertaining eighth novel in this delightful series. Take your seats. The curtain is going up on the Fairy — Sugar Plum that is, clumsy mice, malfunctioning toys, and murder!

Made in the USA
Columbia, SC
06 January 2023

75671799R00120